The Road to Farringale

Modern Magick, 1

Charlotte E. English

1

THE TROLL WAS NOT especially large, as trolls go: six feet and a bit, maybe seven at most. He had a run-down look about him, like he hadn't washed in a while and had no plans to do so anytime soon. He wore a ratty zip-up jumper with the air of a charity-shop purchase about it; had it been only second-hand when he'd bought it, or already third? Its faded navy colour did nothing for his sallow complexion, and the tracksuit bottoms and trainers he wore with it were no better. His bulbous eyes rested a moment upon me, took in my coiffed hair and silk dress, then shifted to my colleague, Jay, who stood nervously unsmiling beside me.

I expected an enquiry of some kind. A greeting, maybe, or even a challenge. But he said nothing; only stared at us with dull, incurious expectation.

I tried to look past him into the Enclave, but he'd opened the stone slab of the door only just wide enough to talk to us. Obstructive. Not a good sign. 'Morning,' I said brightly, and it *was* a bright morning: mid-April and balmy, sun high in the sky and rosily smiling. A perfect day for a drive into the hills. 'We're from the Society for Magickal Heritage,' I told him, using my official voice. 'We have received word of a pair of unregistered alikats in these parts. Would you know anything about that?'

The troll's answer was to slam the door on us, setting up a fine, booming echo that reverberated along the grassy hillside.

'He knows nothing,' Jay translated.

'They never do.' I stepped back from the door, or what had once been the door, and surveyed it speculatively. Now it appeared to be nothing but a slab of bare stone in a rocky cliff face, patches of heathery grass scattered above and before it. We were deep in the Yorkshire Moors, not far from the town of Helmsley (or so Jay informed me). I wondered if the powers back Home knew how far the South Moors Troll Enclave had deteriorated. Considering the state of their Doorkeeper, the signs were unpromising.

'Ves,' said Jay, eyeing me. 'What are you doing?'

'I am wondering if there is another way in.'

'There won't be another *legal* way in. You know the rules.'

I rolled my eyes. Jay was only a few years younger than me, I judged, so he was no wide-eyed intern. But he *was* fresh from the Hidden University. The tutors there spend a lot of time drilling the students in The Rules, of which there are many. For example, one does not chatter about magickal stuff to those without the Vision to see it for themselves. And, one does not visit the private spaces of Hidden Communities without their express invitation, which means one is only allowed to use their front door. *With* one of the residents on the other side of it, politely holding it open.

'All very true,' I said. 'But that's the official policy. In our line of work, it is sometimes necessary to bend the rules a bit.'

'Aren't there complaints?'

I smiled mirthlessly. 'They try that, once in a while. It rarely ends well. In this instance, I'm pretty sure these fine folk are illegally holding at least two alikats, and if it's a breeding pair that's even worse. How are they going to report us for misdemeanours without revealing their own transgressions?'

Jay narrowed his deep brown eyes at me. 'That does not make it all right to freely break all the Rules.'

'No? How else would you like to get those kats out of there, then? I make it about half an hour before the first one gets eaten.'

'I'm sure we can come up with... wait. Eaten?'

I couldn't help sighing. These fresh graduates, so... naive. 'Why do you think Trolls are generally discouraged from keeping alis?'

'Because... because alikats are considered endangered.'

Jay obviously hadn't thought that one through. 'Exactly.'

'Ah.' Jay stopped arguing and joined me in searching for a way in. We proceeded to spend half an hour or so inspecting the hillside for something conveniently resembling a back door, and came up with nothing. We ended up back in front of that stone portal, which was still firmly closed.

'Oh well,' said I. 'We'll have to do it the fun way.'

'The fun way?'

'I, um. I meant the questionable way.'

Jay folded his arms and stared me down. 'After you, then.' I do not know why he insists on wearing leather jackets but I do wish he would not; they suit him far too well.

I rang the bell again. It wasn't a bell at all, in the usual way of those things, but the expression's apt enough. I laid my right hand, palm-flat, against the stone and politely requested entrance.

As per the Magickal Accords, the inhabitants of the South Moors Troll Enclave — if they weren't known to be in Recluse — were pretty much honour bound to answer the door. They were required to co-operate with Jay and I as well, of course, but that hadn't held much weight with them, so who knew? Jay and I waited in hope, and our patience was rewarded. Eventually. About four long minutes later, a thread of dull topaz light raced around the cliff face, tracing the outline of a door, and that door creaked open.

They had changed their Doorkeeper. Mr. Tracksuit and Trainers was nowhere in evidence; replacing him was a larger, lumpier, and rather more belligerent fellow — no, *lady* — who wasted no time whatsoever in demonstrating how matters stood between us. She bared her yellow teeth and I waited for the spectacular roar of displeasure, most likely preparatory to tearing off our heads, which would undoubtedly follow.

Trolls have a certain reputation, do they not? Not only among those with the Vision to see them. Even the Magicless tell stories like The Three Billy Goats Gruff, in which trolls are hideous beasts who'll eat practically anything.

Usually, they are wrong. I've encountered trolls whose manners, tastes and general refinement would put the finest of the British aristocracy to shame. Trolls whose delight in beauty, culture and the arts go virtually unrivalled across the world; trolls whose academic aptitude and scholastic achievements far exceed my own.

Then again, I have periodically encountered the other sort, too. The ones the Norwegians were talking about when they began telling that story about the Gruffs. *Those* trolls really will eat almost anything, provided it's fresh, and in a pinch that would certainly include yours truly.

So I had to forgive Jay for his obvious unease, faced as he was with a displeased Doorkeeper who possibly hadn't eaten for an hour or two. He backed away, leaving me to face the good lady alone.

In his defence, it did look like an involuntary step back. Those survival instincts, they'll put paid to your manly courage any day of the week.

Fortunately, nothing put paid to mine. I smiled my nicest smile at the Doorkeeper — who had not, after all, chosen to treat us to a vocal display of displeasure — and said, in my friendliest tone, 'We'd really like to come in. Just a quick visit, nothing to—'

I stopped because the Doorkeeper was opening her mouth. She was probably preparing to shout at us, or roar at us, or something of the kind, though her movements were peculiarly slow. It seemed to cost her a lot of effort merely to part her lips, which was odd indeed, but convenient because it presented me with a wide open mouth to throw my neighbourly offering into. My gift was a tiny pearl of a thing, all pale, lustrous beauty and lethal potential.

Well, not really lethal. It was a sleep draught, the kind of thing that was once served oddly-coloured and bubbling in peculiar glass jars. The technicians at Home have started compressing them into these bead forms instead. It's the same potency, only smaller, and easier to deliver. Every bit as fast-acting, though; the jelly-type shell that holds everything together dissolves in the mouth in seconds.

It took only slightly longer than that for the Door-keeper to evince a promising swaying upon her boot-clad feet.

'Back a bit more,' I warned Jay, who'd begun to show signs of plucking up his courage for an advance. I wandered back a bit myself, and waited.

The troll pitched forward, and landed upon her face. All ten feet of her hit the ground with a *thud*, which resonated so powerfully I was even moved to hurry a little.

'In we go,' I said, and grabbed Jay by the arm. 'You can study her later, if you like, but just now we need to get on with the job.'

'I don't want to study her,' Jay retorted, pulling his arm out of my grip. 'I was just interested. I've never seen a troll like her before.'

'You can admire her later, too. Maybe she'll take your phone number.'

'I didn't mean—'

'Alikats,' I reminded him. 'Quickly.'

He muttered something inaudible, then added snidely: 'I just find it hard to take you seriously with that hair.'

I tossed the hair in question, undaunted. Just because it was cerulean-blue, and arranged in impossibly perfect ringlets; did that give him any excuse to question my authority, or my expertise? 'I know you are jealous, and I can't blame you, but this is only our first assignment together and I'd like to survive it intact. If you help me retrieve these kats without anybody losing a limb, I'll get you a Curiosity all of your own. A wardrobe that spawns a new, jazzy leather jacket every morning, say. Or a mirror that shows only your best features.'

All Jay's features are his best features, in fairness. He flicked his pretty, pretty eyes at me in annoyance — they're the colour of dark chocolate, those eyes, and they have that velvety quality, too. It's all decidedly unfair, and I can't decide yet whether or not he knows it. 'Lead on,' he said, choosing (perhaps wisely) to ignore my facetiousness.

I led.

The Enclave proved to be much as I expected: a jumbled mess. The town was built in circles —

they do like curves, trolls — and formed of tall, imposing block stone houses built in sinuous lines. Those houses were probably handsome, once, but they'd been allowed to deteriorate. Some of them had lost their original carved oaken doors, and had others tacked on in place; the new ones looked as though they'd been ripped off some shoebox of a concrete dwelling, probably from a local housing estate. Nothing had been painted in at least ten years. Rubbish lay stacked in piles in every corner, and discarded refuse lined the cobbled stone pathways.

The aroma of the place might best be termed Unpleasant. Let's leave it at that.

There weren't too many residents about, which was fortunate for us, though I wondered where everybody was. I saw a few listless-looking souls trudging purposelessly hither and thither, their heads covered with cheap knitted hats. They wore the same fashion of frayed, mismatched clothes as the Doorkeepers.

Nobody stopped us. I'd half expected the noise of the Doorkeeper's fall to attract some kind of attention, but either they had not heard (was that possible? The woman fell like a *tree!*) or they did not care. Nor did they question the sudden appearance of a pair of humans, one all improbably-coloured hair and spectacular fashion sense, the other all cinnamon skin, chocolate eyes and tousled cuteness (should I stop making Jay sound edible...? Okay then). I suppose they had no particular reason to interfere with us. If they were unaware of what we'd done to their Doorkeeper, they'd assume we had been given clearance to enter.

It did not take us long to find out what had become of the alikats. The Enclave was eerily quiet; the sound of a distressed yowl carried nicely. Jay and I veered as one, and made for the alikats at a run.

There proved to be a little square in the centre of the town (or shall I call it a round? For it, like everything else in the place, was pleasingly curvaceous). A cluster of trolls had gathered in an eager knot around a fire pit — or what passed for eager around here; they were at least visibly breathing, which gave them the edge over the rest of the townspeople. The leader of this little group was unquestionably the hunch-backed one in the middle, whose broad shoulders and massive hands looked more than capable of ripping me to pieces. He held a cleaver. To his left stood a troll in a candy-striped jumper that looked like it was knitted by somebody's grandmother. For his convenience, she was obligingly holding out one of our missing alikats. The poor creature's indigo-shaded fur bristled with fright, and it fought mightily to free itself, but to no avail; nothing could dislodge the fierce grip in which it was held.

I noticed that its captor had painted her finger-nails a charming cerise, which was a nice effort, even if the lacquer was rather chipped.

'See the other one?' I asked of Jay as we approached.

'Nope. You do this, I'll do that.' He veered off, went around the knot of trolls and disappeared.

I didn't argue, even though his desertion left me to deal with six or eight trolls unaided. Two alikats were missing, only one was in evidence; I felt a stab of fear, for those kats are more than merely *endangered.* Like many magickal creatures, they feed off magickal energies (in a manner of speaking), and there are blessed few of those bouncing around nowadays. Things were different back in, say, the middle ages. In those days, practically everybody was Magickal and alikats, and all their ilk, were a dime a dozen — or comparatively, anyway. Here in the early twenty-first century... well. I can't even guess at the approximate value of a breeding pair of alis, they are *that* rare. The Powers would have my head if Jay and I returned with only one.

And these idiots were trying to *eat* them.

'Stop!' I barked. The trolls' absolute obliviousness to my presence — and Jay's — was curious, and I had to repeat the word twice more at increasing volume before one of them finally looked up at me. This alert, lively specimen fixed his muddy grey eyes upon me with a dull spark of awareness, and nudged the hunchback.

But too late, because that cleaver was already swinging down, aimed unerringly for the yowling alikat's neck.

2

DAMNIT.

I threw caution and dignity to the winds and made a leap for the alikat. We fell in a blur of flying hair and fur and deeply unhappy beast, and I'm pretty sure that cleaver missed my shoulders by a mere two inches but it was *worth it,* because I came up with an armful of kat. The creature was hissing and writhing like a mad thing but she was, blessedly, still alive.

'Right,' I snapped, eyeing the hunchback with all the justifiable anger of a woman who has only narrowly escaped death by cleaver. He stared back at me with the same dull lack of interest as the rest of his kin, which took the proverbial wind out of my sails just a little. 'Society,' I said firmly, and my identifying symbol (a purple unicorn against the

Society's backdrop of three crossed wands) flashed briefly in the air before me. I fear the dignity of the moment was somewhat impaired by the antics of my rescuee, which continued to thrash and claw at me as though *I* was its tormentor. Honestly, did the absurd creature not realise I had saved its skin? I tightened my grip upon it, trying to ignore the way its black claws sank deeper into my poor flesh, and lifted my chin haughtily. 'The Rules for possession, care and treatment of Magickal Creatures are well known to you, are they not? And upon this point, they are *very* clear. No endangered species may be owned without a valid permit, and they are *never* to be put on the menu!'

I expected some manner of objection to be raised to this, if to nothing else that I had done. But the hunchback only stared at me for several long seconds, mouth slightly agape. Then, finally, he shrugged, letting his dirty cleaver drop heedlessly onto the cobbled stone square at his feet. The sharp clatter of its fall split the heavily silent air with a *crack*, and I jumped.

The hunchback made no attempt either to defend his conduct, or to reassert his ownership of the alikat. Instead, he turned away and shambled off, his candy-striped companion shuffling after. One by one, the other half-dozen trolls scattered, leaving me alone in the square. I watched them go, stunned.

There was definitely something odd going on. Why were the trolls so apathetic? What had prompted them to try to make a dinner of an alikat? They *did* know the Rules. These policies had been in place for many years.

The quiet at least gave me an opportunity to pacify my poor alikat. I gentled it with a little charm I learned from my mother — handy when I was a child, she once said, which does not speak well of my temperament at that age, but never mind. The kat relaxed in my arms, affording me with the leisure to observe the toll its understandable distress had taken upon me. My arms were striped with stinging wounds that oozed trickles of blood into the shredded sleeves of my lovely silk dress, and I could not hold back a sigh. This line of work is, all too often, fatal to skin and clothes alike.

Jay reappeared. To my vast relief, he was carrying the other alikat. Definitely a male, this one: it was half again the size of the little female that now lay so quiescent in my arms, its fur dappled in deeper shades of indigo and black. To my mingled admiration and disgust, the second alikat embraced Jay as though the two had been best friends since their earliest youth. It lay twined around Jay's neck and half down one of his arms, its whiskers vibrating with the force of its purr. I detected no signs of injury in Jay, though the thick leather of his jacket might have had something to do with that.

He took stock of my bloodied state and the alikat lying in my arms, and gave a tiny, satisfied nod. I tried not to feel offended by his visible lack of concern for the fate of my poor arms. 'Vaporised the lot?' he guessed, glancing around at the empty square.

'Nothing but dust and ash.'

He grinned. 'What did you really do with them?'

'Nothing. They submitted to my withdrawal of the alikat without a murmur, and left.'

Jay's brows went up. 'Odd.'

'Very. Shall we take these poor little soldiers home?'

'Lead on.'

'Uh, no. You lead on.'

Jay gave me a tiny salute. 'You are the boss.'

'Fine.' I cast a quick look around to get my bearings, and set off.

'That's the wrong way,' Jay helpfully observed.

I stopped. 'Remember why they assigned you to me?'

'I just... didn't think you could really be that bad.' Jay picked a direction almost the opposite of the one I had been wandering in, and marched off.

'I'd love to take offence,' I said as I fell in behind him. 'But the truth is, I couldn't find my way out of a bucket.'

'Noted.' Jay sounded perfectly composed. Not a quiver of mirth could I detect.

'Are you laughing at me?'

'Never.'

'You are.'

His shoulders began to shake, which prompted a dissatisfied *mrow* from his alikat. 'Yes. Yes, I am.'

I caught up with Jay, and expressed my disapproval with a disdainful toss of my cerulean curls. 'I have other talents.'

'I am sure you do.'

'Aren't you going to ask what they are?'

'I've been told what they are. Vast knowledge of magickal history. Specialised knowledge of ancient spells, beasts and artefacts. No insignificant skill with charms.'

'Great hair.'

'*Great* hair.'

I smiled, mollified. 'What are your talents?'

'I,' said Jay, 'can find my way out of a bucket.'

'I am speechless with admiration.'

'*And* the South Moors Troll Enclave. There's the door.'

BURDENED AS WE'D HOPED to be by a pair of frightened (and possibly injured) animals, we had judged it best to eschew flight this time and travel by car. At least, this was the official motive. I prefer cars anyway, for two reasons. One: it is unnecessary to manage the thorny problem of finding one's way to somewhere while maintaining an invisibility or deflection glamour, all without falling off one's choice of steed (chairs are popular). And two: call it vanity, but I hate what the high winds do to my hair. Cars, of course, have heating and sat nav and roofs overhead, which is delightful of them. They also have traffic jams, but I consider that a price worth paying for comfort.

Since Jay would be driving, he had insisted we use his car. I'd half expected it to be some kind of zippy, sporty thing with too few seats and overly glossy paintwork, but instead he drove a shabby-looking Ford Something in a respectable shade of dark red. It displayed the kinds of scratches and minor dents suggestive of a car that is well-used but not quite so well-loved. We carefully loaded our (thankfully uninjured) alis into a pair of cat carriers, settled them in the back, and headed for Home.

When I say "Home", I mean headquarters. The Society for Magickal Heritage is officially called The Society for the Preservation and Protection of Magickal Heritage, or SPPMH for short. But while lengthy and convoluted acronyms might work beautifully for, say, the RSPCA, we summarily rejected the garbling and spitting involved and opted for the serene simplicity of merely: The Society. And the Society is housed in a gorgeous country mansion which is, considering its size, surprisingly hard to find.

We like it that way. The house has no official name; that's why we just call it "Home". Like the Hidden University, it isn't marked on any map. It has no website, and no sat nav will direct you to it. This, as you may imagine, has frequently caused me no little difficulty. I was two days late for my first day of work.

The house dates from the mid seventeenth century. It was once owned by one of the more prominent magickal families among the nobility of England and Ireland, so they say, though reports vary as to which family it was. Officially, it was knocked down after the Second World War, like so many of our country houses; this piece of misdirection, combined with a liberal application of deterrent charms, keeps us largely secure from the outside world. It drowses, quietly hidden, somewhere near the border of South Yorkshire and Derbyshire, ringed by peaceful hills, and as wholly unspoilt as a building that's Home to two hundred people can possibly be.

Not being directionally impaired, Jay got us there within a couple of hours. I felt so many things upon approaching that beautiful house, as I always do. Admiration for its rambling stonework, its fanciful little towers, its long windows, parapets and soaring archways. Fondness, for the place I've called home for more than a decade. Pride, for the work we do; we've saved and restored countless books and artefacts; rescued many species of magickal creatures from the disaster of extinction; tracked down and extracted magickal Treasures and Curiosities without number, sometimes from situations of considerable danger. What kind of work could be more important than that?

This array of warm feelings suffered an early check. As we drove slowly up the spacious driveway, I noticed that Zareen had turned the flanking rows of stately, centuries-old oak trees upside down. Again.

'Is it too soon to revoke her Curiosity privileges?' I sighed, wincing at the exposed roots sagging helplessly in the air.

'It appears to be too late,' said Jay.

'It's never too late.'

'You'll have to talk to Milady. She—'

A great, groaning *creaking* sound interrupted whatever Jay was about to add, as the tree nearest to us flipped right-side-up again. Dislodged earth rained down upon the car like a shower of hail, and I was thankful anew that we had not come swooping in upon a pair of inconveniently open-topped chairs.

'*Definitely* talk to Milady,' growled Jay, narrowly avoiding a falling clot of earth of alarming size with a neat swerve of the wheels.

It was good to be Home.

JAY WAS ONLY RECRUITED by the Society a couple of weeks ago, and it shows.

We parked, retrieved our alikats and made for the house. I was aiming for a side door that would take us straight into the Magickal Creatures wing, but as we approached, the little green-painted portal faded into the stonework and disappeared.

I stepped back.

'Uh,' said Jay, blinking and pointing at where the door had been. 'Is... it supposed to do that?'

'No, but all attempts to dissuade it have failed. I think Milady's given up. Take a step back, Jay.'

'What?'

I don't know whether it was the vanishing door that did it or the inverted trees beforehand, but Jay definitely wasn't at his sharpest. I grabbed him and *pulled*, just as an elegant spiral staircase made from solid wrought iron descended from above, slamming into the ground a little too close to where Jay had been standing moments before.

3

J AY STARED AT THE staircase in consternation.

'Thanks,' he said faintly.

I made a flourishing gesture of invitation, indicating the proffered stairs with a sweep of my free arm. 'After you.'

'Uh. Why don't you go first?'

'Don't worry, the House won't hurt you.'

Jay gave me the are-you-crazy stare. 'I've narrowly missed having my car crushed by a ball of earth the size of four of my heads, almost been flattened by a flying set of stairs, and all of this has happened in the last ten minutes of my life.'

'All right. *I'll* go first.' I picked up my discarded creature carrier and set off up the steps. After a few moments' hesitation, I heard Jay's footsteps ringing behind me.

There was no door at the top, but there was a long window set with many small panes of glass. When I reached the top, about fifty of those panes flickered and vanished, creating an entryway just large enough to admit Jay and myself.

'Thank you,' I said. 'How convenient.' For beyond the makeshift doorway I could see one of the larger, oak-panelled drawing-rooms of the first floor, or what had been a drawing-room once. It was now used as a kind of common room, and one of its occupants was Miranda Evans, our vet and specialist in magickal beasts of all kinds.

'Hi,' I said as I wandered through the window, and set the creature carrier down at her feet.

She was lounging in the kind of shabby, velvet-clad wing-back chair in which Home abounds, her red robes partially open to reveal a chunky hand-knitted jumper worn underneath. Her blonde hair was half out of its bindings, as usual; she took one look at me and Jay and the present we'd brought for her, and immediately scraped it back into a more business-like ponytail. 'More work,' she said with her quirk of a smile. 'Lovely.'

'Alikats, breeding pair. Extracted from South Moors.'

Her brows went up at that, and she hastily swallowed the dregs of her cup of tea. 'Injuries?'

'None visible. I think they're unharmed, they just need a check-up and then resettling.'

By the time I had finished this sentence, Miranda was already on her knees, peeking through the bars at my slumbering alikat. 'Gorgeous,' she commented.

I'd lost her attention altogether, but that was all right. Jay and I watched as she gathered up our beleaguered pair; with a nod to us both, she left the common room at a smartish pace.

Jay glanced behind himself. The door we'd used had sealed itself up again, turning back into a window. 'Is it a coincidence that we found Miranda right here?'

'No,' I said, making a beeline for the kettle and the tea cupboard. 'That was the House helping us out. It does that.'

'When it isn't trying to kill us.'

'It wasn't trying to kill us.'

'Yeah, right.'

'It was trying to kill *you*. *I* was fine.'

This was a joke, of course, but I regretted it when Jay developed an expression of mingled anxiety and affront. I put a cup of tea into his hands to pacify him, or at least to distract him, neither of which worked. 'Haven't you seen the House do that before?'

'Nope.'

'It's because you're new,' I decided. 'It hasn't figured you out yet. It will soon.'

'Then it will stop trying to kill me?' Jay looked profoundly sceptical.

'No. Then you'll stop being careless enough to get in the way of House's helpful gestures. Or Zareen's pranks, for that matter.'

Jay took a long gulp of tea, like a man chugging something strong and alcoholic. 'Survive a few more weeks for optimum results. Got it.'

I chugged mine, too, for we did not have time to linger. Somewhat to my regret, for the first-floor common room is one of my favourite places at Home. It's something to do with the quality of the light, I think; those long windows somehow admit the perfect degree of it, in the perfect quantity, keeping the room bathed in a peaceful glow that perfectly brings out the mellow tones of the wooden walls and flooring. Those chairs are remarkable, too. We might not have had time, but I sank into one of them anyway, the crimson one. Its proportions immediately adjusted around me, creating of itself a seat of perfect size and dimensions to accommodate my frame. The cushions softened, too, since I prefer a pillowy structure, and the back shortened a little to suit my height — its previous occupant was apparently rather taller than me, which isn't unusual.

'Lovely,' I said, wearing my smile of serene contentment.

'Out you get,' said Jay unsympathetically. 'We've a report to make.'

I sighed, deeply, but he was right. Something was very much amiss at South Moors, and the Powers needed to know about it right away. 'Fine, fine,' I said with decided ill grace. I threw a cushion at him as I rose; unlike the loose earth from Zareen's inverted trees, *this* he dodged with easy grace, and raised a single brow at me.

'Have you *no* mischievous side?' I asked him in exasperation.

'None whatsoever.' He said it with such a straight face, I had to believe him.

'You and Zareen should get on like—'

'Cats and dogs,' he interrupted. 'We do.'

I tossed the tangles from my hair, adjusted my poor ruined dress, and made for the door. 'They should have given you someone *much* more serious to work with.'

'But you're the one who needed me.' Jay somehow beat me to the door, opened it, and held it for me with an ironical little bow.

Considering the most prominent of the reasons why I needed him, that reflection was mildly embarrassing, so I responded only with a haughty look of disdain and strode forth.

Jay was kind enough to fall in behind me without further comment, and I was able to pretend that I didn't hear the low chuckle that was *almost* masked by the sound of the door closing behind us.

THE PROCESS FOR SEEKING an audience with Milady is rather particular.

First, one is expected to present oneself in her preferred location, that being at the very top of the very tallest tower of the House. And why not? There is something agreeably fairy tale about it, even if the physical exertion required is not always well received by her supplicants.

Jay managed the ascent of three narrow, winding stone staircases in increasingly strained silence. They are the kind with uneven steps (charmingly worn by time, and the passage of a million footsteps); spiralling construction (tightly wound, so as to make of them the greatest possible obstacle); and occasional landings, randomly dispersed (the kind with dark, shadowy corners, wherein one half expects to find all manner of disagreeable creatures residing). And of course, none of them has fewer than thirty or so steps. All things considered, I was impressed that he made it halfway up the fourth staircase before the complaints began.

'Isn't there a lift?' He sounded faintly breathless but not excessively so, which wasn't bad. Jay obviously kept himself decently fit.

'Of course not,' I said, in the ringing tones of a supremely fit woman (a boast, but what can I say? I've been climbing these staircases every day for more than a decade. That alone will give a woman lungs of steel, and the hind quarters of a racehorse).

'What do you mean, *of course not*? Lifts are wonderful.'

I cast him a withering look over my shoulder. 'This is a seventeenth-century mansion. Where do you suggest we put an elevator? Which priceless and irreplaceable features shall we rip out in order to make room for it?'

'Fair point. What about the house itself, then? If it can present you with a staircase straight up to the common room, it can whisk us up to the top tower in a jiffy.'

'Are you in a wheelchair, Jay?'

'Uh... no.'

'Valerie Greene — have you met her yet? Library? — is wheelchair-bound. Dear House takes the very best care of *her*. Any door she approaches opens upon just the place she wants to go.'

'That's good of it.'

'Isn't it? And quite ingenious.'

'So we're left to haul ourselves up all these stairs because...?'

'Because we are able-bodied, fit young people, Jay, and I don't think House approves of laziness.'

I fancy it was the word *laziness* that silenced him, or perhaps he simply ran out of breath. Either way, he had not another word to advance until we arrived at the top of the sixth set of stairs and stood, briefly winded (or he was, at any rate; I deny all such charges), and taking great gulps of air. We were in a cramped, rounded tower; before us was one of those narrow, arrow-slit type windows filled in with glass, through which we were afforded a fine view of the green, sun-dappled hills beyond the gates.

'Lovely,' I commented.

Jay said nothing, so I turned to the one other feature of that stark little tower: a heavy oak door, closed and barred.

I knocked.

'What now?' whispered Jay, when nothing happened.

'House is consulting with Milady as to whether she wants to admit us.'

'Does she ever decline?'

'Me, no. You, however... who knows.'

Jay allowed that to pass in silence. 'Does she really live up *here*?' he said after a while — just as the door unbarred itself with a *clang* and swung slowly inwards.

'In a manner of speaking.' Jay made no move, so I entered the room first.

Milady's room is only about six metres across, its walls curved most of the way around. Those walls were fitted with panelling at some point in history, though not with the smooth, warm-hued oak that's prevalent across most of the House. The tower's walls are sheathed in iridescent crystal. There's one window, but it doesn't look over the countryside like the one in the antechamber. Through it one can see only swirling white mist.

I stepped into the centre of the room, and positioned myself in the middle of the thick, royal-blue rug that covers the floor.

'Afternoon, Milady,' I said cordially, and curtseyed.

'Uh.' Jay came up next to me and turned a full circle on the spot, neck craning, as though Milady might be hidden somewhere in a room with no furniture and no corners. 'Where is she?' he whispered to me.

I elbowed him. 'Say hello,' I hissed.

'Hello, Milady.'

That was it. I elbowed him again, a bit harder this time, and by way of judicious application of pressure to his upper back I contrived to force him into a semblance of a polite bow.

The air sparkled. 'Cordelia Vesper,' said a low, cultured female voice. 'Jay Patel. What have you to tell me today?'

4

NOTHING EVER WORRIES MILADY. I could tell her an army of hostile magicians was advancing upon the House with a legion of direbeasts in tow, and she would merely say, 'Unfortunate. Very well,' dispense a simple, efficient plan for containing the problem which would work perfectly, and then invite us all for tea afterwards.

She heard our account of the South Moors Troll Enclave in thoughtful silence, a silence she maintained for some ten or fifteen seconds after I had finished speaking. That, it seems, was as much time as she required to consider our information, place it in context, and devise her response.

'You did well to retrieve the alikats,' she said. 'There are but twelve breeding pairs left in England, at least that are known. We could not easily bear to lose one of them. They are in Miranda's care?'

'Yes, Milady.'

'Then they will be well tended to. Regarding the trolls, their behaviour is cause for concern. I will arrange for a consultant to meet with you. He will be here this afternoon.'

This was vague, but I knew by then that Milady's plans always became clear soon enough, so I curtseyed again and murmured something agreeing. Jay gave me the side-eye, and said nothing.

'Return to me once you have met with my consultant, for I shall have a new assignment for you this evening. Jay Patel.'

The name was spoken in a tone so indistinguishable from the rest, it took Jay a moment to realise he was being addressed. 'Yes?' he said hesitantly.

'This was your first assignment with Vesper. Are you contented with her?'

Privately I thought that Milady might have done better to ask this question of Jay when I was not standing right next to him, but he took it in stride. 'We work well enough together, Milady,' he replied.

'Very well. Vesper?'

I thought of the hesitancy he had shown when faced with even the apathetic trolls of South Moors. I had wondered a little about his courage, but that was probably unfair of me. He was new. If he had met any trolls at the Hidden University, it might well have been limited to old Maj, professor of anthropology, and she was ancient, wizened, soft-spoken and totally unintimidating. He had faltered, but he'd held. He would get used to it. 'I am happy to continue our partnership,' I said. 'We made it through the mission without getting even a little bit lost, and I can't remember the last time that has happened to me.'

'He is more than your chauffeur, Vesper.'

'I know that,' said I hastily. Did I though? It occurred to me that I knew little about Jay's specific abilities, and the only reason Milady had given for assigning him to accompany me was my deplorable tendency to lose my way — besides his obvious need for basic induction to the Society, of course, which anybody might have provided him with. It did not much surprise me to learn that there was more to Milady's thinking than that, but as to what it *was,* I was in the dark.

No matter. This, too, would become clear in time.

'You will find chocolate in the pot,' said Milady, which befuddled Jay but I knew it for one of her characteristic, mild dismissals. I made a final curtsey, motioned Jay into a parting bow, and hustled both of us out of the tower room.

Jay was silent all the way down four staircases. Then he said: '*What?*'

'To what are you referring?'

'All of it.'

'More specifically?'

'Let's begin with: who exactly is Milady?'

'No idea,' I said brightly.

Jay stopped, and stared at me.

'Nobody does,' I said with a shrug. 'Some say she's the latest scion of the aristocratic family who built this House, which makes sense. Some say she is the *same* woman who built this House, which is less likely, as she'd have to be centuries old. But who knows? She could be either of those things, or neither. We know her as the founder and benefactor of the Society, She Who Pulls Our Strings, the Bosslady, and that's enough for most of us.'

'Why is she a disembodied voice?'

'I don't know.'

'Why did you keep curtseying to a disembodied voice?'

'Oh, I'm sure she can see us. That window, I think, though I'm not sure how.'

'You don't think that curtseying is a little old-fashioned?'

'So's Milady.'

Jay sighed, and ran a hand through his hair. 'You know, when I got this job offer, they told me. At the University. They *told* me it was strange up here.'

'They weren't wrong.' We'd made it back to the first floor by then; I steered Jay back to the common room, where, as promised, we found a welcome addition to its equipment. An oversized, eighteenth-century silver chocolate-pot stood upon one of the tables, wisps of steam curling invitingly from its spout. A pair of chocolate-drinking cups had been set beside; these, of course, were the delicate, porcelain kind, with gilding around the rims.

'You are kidding me,' said Jay in blank disbelief.

I took a seat and poured out chocolate for both of us. It was sweet and spiced, dark and rich, pure luxury: exactly the way we don't drink it anymore. 'Have a bit,' I encouraged Jay. 'One tends to feel better afterwards.' And I did, already, even after only a few sips. I was less tired, less hungry, and the scratches striping my arms were already stinging less.

Jay did not believe me, clearly — not until he had drunk half of his share of the chocolate.

'Strange but good?' I invited him to allow.

He drained his cup and poured out another. 'Strange,' he said with emphasis.

I raised a brow, and waited. Sure enough, a reluctant smile crossed his face and he sank back into his chair with a sigh, visibly more relaxed than he had been half an hour earlier. 'Strange but good,' he conceded.

WE WERE AT LEISURE to amuse ourselves for the next two or three hours. I spent the time changing my ruined blue dress for a printed cotton one in spring-like rose, worn with a light shawl. It clashed with my cerulean hair, so I employed my wonderful Curiosity — a ring, this one, with a charm embedded — and adjusted the latter to a more complementary blue-lavender hue.

I don't know what Jay did. We separated after we had finished with Milady's chocolate, and did not reconvene until we were called to meet the consultant. I made my way back down to the soaring, marble-floored entrance hall to find Jay already waiting, jacket discarded. He wore jeans, and a simple pale blue cotton shirt which contrived to look simultaneously neat and lightweight and casual. I approved.

My admiration was not mutual, for Jay looked me over and said: 'You look like a bouquet of flowers.' The words sounded complimentary enough, but he

spoke them so tonelessly, his face so expression-
less, that I could not help concluding that some
unspoken criticism lay behind them.

So I ignored this.

'Where—' I began, for the hall was empty other
than the two of us; no sign of our promised consultant could I discern. But as I spoke, Nell — Nell De-
laney, of media and tech and suchlike — stuck her
exquisitely greying head around one of the doors
and said: 'Ves? Convention Chamber. He's waiting.'

That made me raise my brows, for that particular
room is arguably the finest at Home. It's usually
used for large gatherings of the significant kind. We
only put individuals in there if they're important,
and we want to impress them. Not, of course, if
they're the important kind of people we're hoping
will agree to fund us. Such a show of magnificence
would be quite misplaced there. So who had Milady
found to meet us?

I adjusted my hair, checked that my attire was
immaculate, and adopted my most confident stride.
It wouldn't do to appear unsure.

'I don't suppose...?' said Jay, trailing after me.

'Nope,' I said, without waiting for the rest of his
sentence. It didn't matter what he intended to ask
about this afternoon's adventure; I had no more
idea than he did.

The grand double doors of the Convention Chamber had been invitingly flung open, and we were able to walk straight in — stopped only briefly by Robert Foster, who had obviously been given Brawn Duty outside the doors. He's a big man, Robert, and commensurately impressive at all the arts one might wish to employ if any conceivable variety of threat might chance to be mounted in one's vicinity. Or in other words, he's Scary Rob.

'Ves,' he said to me with a nod. He doesn't exactly cultivate the air of a man of force. He favours the neat, plain attire one might adopt to work as, say, a school teacher, or a general practitioner (the latter of which is not misplaced, since he... is). His tightly-curled black hair is always in need of a trim, and I've never seen him with less than three or four days' worth of stubble. But I suppose he has no need to dress the part. You can *feel* the danger in Robert; not by any overt signs of menace, for he is a careful and essentially gentle man. But he is so chock-full of magickal energy — the *strong* kind — that it's hard to miss.

He cast a vaguely suspicious eye over Jay, who stared back.

Silence.

They could be sizing each other up for half the afternoon, and we had no time for that. 'Jay Patel,' I said quickly. 'My new sidekick. He's with me.'

'Wha — I'm not *with* — sidekick?!'

I ignored these incoherent protestations, took Jay's arm, and at Rob's nod — faintly amused, judging from the involuntary curve of his lips — steered Jay into the Convention Chamber.

The room takes my breath away every time I see it, which is not often. If the entrance hall is impressive, the Chamber is staggering. It has the kind of high ceiling which seems to soar on for half of forever, held up by buttresses of the flying type. Everything is marble and exotic wood and crystal and gilding. It doesn't fit with the rest of the House too well, so it's my belief that it is a later addition. As to when, how or why it came into being, however... who knows. I have been trying to get my hands on a history of the House for years, but if such a book exists, it's very hard to find.

Our contact sat at one of the graceful crystalline side tables, one of Milady's chocolate pots set before him. He had been served with the best our kitchens could offer, which made me mildly envious, for those pastries are to die for. I wondered vaguely if he might be disposed to share.

I could see little of the man himself, for he sat partially concealed behind an enormous folio. So absorbed in his book was he, he seemed unaware of our entrance. I had time to note that he was a man of some height and, apparently, strength; the mere weak and feeble amongst us (like me) would have spread that heavy book open upon the table, but he held it up before him with no sign of strain whatsoever.

Good, then. Milady had found us a representative of the troll communities. An important one.

I cleared my throat. 'Good afternoon, sir.'

The book was instantly closed, and set aside. I received an unimpeded view of by far the most gorgeous troll I have ever beheld, and I mean *gorgeous* in the sense of spectacularly well-presented as well as... well, rather handsome. All height and muscle and perfect posture was he, his bulky shoulders encased in a dark blue velvet coat over a silk shirt. He wore a kind of cravat, and an actual top hat lay on the table beside him. A *top hat.* No wonder he and Milady were acquainted. His skin was a pleasing jadeish hue, his features perfect. All this splendour and privilege might lead one to suppose he'd have an attitude problem, but his vivid green eyes twinkled with good humour as he looked the two of us over. His gaze lingered upon the vibrant mass of my hair.

'The famous Vesper,' he said in a low, rich voice. 'I hear much of you.'

5

I THINK IT WAS the word *famous* which rattled Jay, for he transferred his attention from the gorgeously arrayed consultant and blinked incredulously at me. '*Are* you?'

'No,' I said crisply, and then amended that to, 'Not really. Baron Alban flatters me.'

'Only a little,' said the baron, and that twinkle deepened. He fingered his cravat and added, 'How did you guess my name?'

'Your reputation precedes you.' Oh, I'd heard about the baron all right. The Troll Court's ambassador to the Hidden Ministry (the magickal government of England), and a prime favourite everywhere he goes. His reputation for flamboyance far exceeds my own — or shall we say, his notoriety? He is also known for his wit, his cleverness and his knowledge of magickal creatures, history and communities, but people don't talk about any of that so much as they talk of his hats, his coats and (by rumour at least) his ladies. I'd wanted to meet him for years.

I was still surprised, though, to find him at the House. When Milady had spoken of a "consultant", I had at least half expected a troll, but I had pictured... what? A scholar like myself, perhaps; someone who was several years into an exhaustive study of troll customs, habits and history, to be published in about fifteen years' time. An anthropologist, a psychologist, a folklorist... *anybody* but Baron Alban.

Since he had made no move to get up and did not appear to wish to stand on ceremony, I took a chair and a cup of chocolate. 'What can we do for you?' I said.

Jay followed my example, but he was wary. I could see that in the rigidity of his posture as he sat across from me, looking ready to run at a moment's notice.

This amused the baron all the more, and he grinned. 'I understand there is a problem at South Moors.'

'Milady spoke of a *consultant.*' I laid a slight emphasis on the last word, hoping my tone would convey a polite question rather than incredulity.

'So I am. I was not born into a barony, you know, and I certainly was not appointed to the post of ambassador at birth. I spent many years of my youth as a rootless vagabond with a tendency to get myself thrown out of every town I lived in, which had its drawbacks. But since I developed an unusually broad knowledge of troll life across most of its strata, it has, on occasion, made me a useful person to consult.'

He spoke with the smoothness, the confidence and the vocabulary of a highly educated man, so I guessed that these rootless, drifting years had been followed by several more of focused study. I wondered what Alban had done to net himself a barony — other than smile gorgeously, which he was doing in my general direction at that very moment.

All right, then.

'What would be your summary of the problem?' Alban asked.

Jay did not seem inclined to lead the way at communicating, which suited me just fine. 'If I had met any of the inhabitants of South Moors individually, I would have said they were... depressed,' I said. 'There is an air of apathy, a greyness, a blankness — though even to call it depression is to state the case too mildly, for they scarcely seemed to hear me when I spoke, and no one vouchsafed any reply. What could possibly afflict a whole village with such symptoms is beyond me to imagine, and I have never heard or read of such a case occurring in history.'

'And the alikats,' Jay put in. 'It is not usual for them to make a meal of such beasts, is it?'

'Not now,' said Alban. 'Some of us will eat just about anything, of course,' — he gave a feral grin as he said this — 'but the Accords have been in place for long enough to deter even a backwater like South Moors from snacking on endangered species.' He winced. 'How many alis were lost?'

'We rescued two,' I said. 'We saw no sign of any others, but who knows what they were eating before word reached us.'

Baron Alban raised his cup to his lips and delicately sipped, silent in thought. The cup ought to have looked tiny and fragile in his huge hands, but it, like the baron's chair, had fitted itself to his proportions. 'Milady was right to summon me,' he finally decided. 'The matter requires the immediate attention of the Court.'

That took the problem neatly out of my hands and Jay's, which was well enough. But I was a little sorry that our meeting with Baron Alban would soon be over, and we would probably never cross paths with him again. I studied him closely, committing points of detail to memory: the exquisite cut of his coat, the sharp points of his superb lapels, that expertly knotted cravat. His sculpted jaw, prominent cheek-bones and wickedly twinkling eyes...

He caught me at this scrutiny and gave me a wink, which, for the sake of my dignity, I pretended not to have observed. Setting down his empty cup, he said: 'I'd like to hear the whole story, please. Every-thing that happened, and everything that you saw.'

This we gave, in as much detail as Jay and I could remember between us. We did a fair job, I think. We are both graduates of the University; we've been taught to observe, and to question. Baron Alban heard us out without interruption, save once or twice to clarify a point of detail. His troubled look deepened as we spoke, and when we were finished he gave a great sigh and rose from his chair. My *goodness,* but he was tall. 'Her Majesty will need to know at once,' he said, gazing down at me with a smile that looked — was it wishful thinking? — a little regretful.

He bowed to us, already taking out his phone, and was gone before I had time to realise that he had given us no insight, no advice, no information at all. But then, he was not there to consult for our benefit; he was there to consult for Milady's.

Jay helped himself to more chocolate — he was swiftly growing to like it, that's for sure — and sat back with a sigh. He had that wide-eyed, flabbergasted look again. 'Strangest day of my life,' he said. 'No contest.'

Poor boy. Little did he know. 'It gets worse.'

'How... how much worse?'

'Or better,' I amended. 'Depends how you look at it.'

Maybe I needed to work on my strategy, for Jay did not look encouraged.

WE WERE BACK IN Milady's tower by nine o'clock upon the following morning. Jay kept his dissatisfaction with the climb to himself this time, which I appreciated, for the morning dawned bright, sunny and beautiful and I wanted to enjoy it. 'Glorious *sun*,' I observed unnecessarily as we toiled up the stairs.

Jay treated this offering with all the interest it deserved, and said nothing.

This time, when we presented ourselves before Milady, Jay bowed without my encouragement. He really *did* like that chocolate.

'Vesper. Jay. Good morning,' said Milady's voice, the air twinkling brightly with every syllable she uttered. 'I hope you are in the mood to travel.'

I perked up at that, for when I am not in the mood to explore? 'Always!' I declared.

Jay's enthusiasm did not quite equal my own. 'Probably,' he allowed.

'You will be familiar with the Farringale Enclave, of course?'

Of *course* I was. Farringale was legend. The site of the Troll Court back in the middle ages, it was renowned for everything — art, scholarship, philosophy, ideas. It was a magickal hub, overflowing with magickal energy; some of the most powerful and most visionary feats of magick ever heard of were developed there, performed there.

Its decline is a sad tale, though not an uncommon one. Time passed, and gradually left Farringale behind. Other schools of magick and ideas supplanted it; other libraries and universities came to be pre-eminent. The Troll Court moved southwards in the early eighteenth century, and Farringale became increasingly isolated from the rest of the world — so much so that there is now considerable debate as to where it is actually situated. Far in the north of England; that is about as much as we can all agree upon. 'Are we going *there*?' I blurted. What a dream! A place steeped in such history, such mystery, such intrigue... what if its legendary libraries were still intact?

'No,' said Milady, and my hopes died. 'You may not be aware that there is suspected to be some key to its decline that is not widely known about, though its precise nature has never been confirmed.'

'Some catastrophe, you mean?'

'Perhaps. Scholars at the Court have traced its deterioration to a mere handful of years, beginning around 1657. In March of that year, the Enclave was thriving. By December, it had shrunk to half its former size. Whether its inhabitants fled or died we do not know, but that there was something gravely amiss is not in doubt.'

'Does Alban suspect a connection with that and the fate of South Moors?' It seemed far-fetched to me, but apparently the baron had access to information I lacked. I felt the familiar envy grow in my breast: a kind of lust for knowledge denied.

Someday I would need to cultivate a connection at the Troll Court, no doubt about that. What other secrets were they hiding in those libraries of theirs?

'It is not an isolated occurrence,' said Milady. 'In 1928, the Garragore Enclave went fully Reclusive. It closed its doors to all outsiders, which is not in itself unusual; but nothing has ever been heard from it again, which is rather more so. It is thought that the settlement faded altogether, and is now barren. But its doors remain sealed, even to the Court. No explanation for its demise has ever been uncovered.'

I'd heard of Garragore as well, though it was nowhere near in the same league as Farringale. Its name appeared in documents from the nineteenth and early twentieth centuries from time to time — mentions in private journals, newspapers, advertisements, that kind of thing. It had not occurred to me to notice that its name had stopped showing up after 1928. I'd had no reason to pay attention to it.

'Are there more such stories?' I asked, feeling slightly sick. Here was a most unpromising pattern.

'There are. Baron Alban is greatly concerned that South Moors may go the way of Farringale and Garragore and the others, if help is not given. But *how* to help is a question no one can yet answer. The baron has requested our assistance.'

'Why?' said Jay. 'Cannot the Troll Court muster the manpower to do it themselves?'

'They are employing their own resources as they see fit. When it comes to the kind of investigation he has in mind, however: we can do it faster.'

'Can we?' I asked. 'How?'

'Because we have Jay.'

That took me aback. Jay? What about him? Alas, my thoughts must have shown on my face, for Jay rolled his eyes at me, his lips twisting in irritation. 'I *am* more than a chauffeur,' he said.

'Oh? What are you?'

Jay's face set into a disgusted expression and he said nothing, so it fell to Milady to explain. 'I re-cruited Jay the moment he was free to join us, for one particular reason. He is a Waymaster.'

Oh.

6

'NOBODY THOUGHT TO MENTION this before?' I asked, unable to suppress a trace of bitterness.

'It was not considered wise to make this ability widely known.'

Waymasters are rare. That is an understatement. One who knows the Ways can make use of all the ancient portals that are spread all over Britain — and indeed, the world. Around here they take the form of henges, for the most part. The big, shiny, popular ones like Stonehenge are never used anymore; too many tourists in the way. But the country is littered with the more humble kind, henges of rock and wood and earth. If you can walk the Ways, you can step from one to another in the blink of an eye. It is an ability that used to be common, but like so much else of magick it has been fading away for generations. Nobody knows why.

I understand that some would find all kinds of interesting, nefarious ways to exploit such an ability as Jay's. But *I* wouldn't. Did they not trust me?

'Jay was assigned to you because you were the best person to train him,' said Milady. 'I wanted you to treat him as an ordinary recruit. I wanted *him* to learn how we manage day by day, with or without a Waymaster to hand, for he will not always have the ability freely at his disposal. It was not intended that you should be kept in the dark about it forever.'

I did not feel much mollified, but I kept my dissatisfaction to myself. It is unprofessional to put one's irritations on display. 'Very well.'

'What would you like us to do?' asked Jay.

'Baron Alban is well-travelled, and frequently visits the more populous and central Enclaves. He is not concerned about the well-being of any of those. There are a few far-flung or mildly reclusive settlements, however, whose fate is more in question. I need you to discover whether they are showing any signs of decay, like South Moors, or any unusual behaviour.'

A mission that proposed to take me all over the country in a trice, and gave me the opportunity to explore several places I had never before visited, could only be welcome to me. 'Yes ma'am!' I said with enthusiasm.

'Thrice the usual budget, Ves,' added Milady, 'and take whatever you need from Stores. You have one week.'

Resources: Great. Time: Less so. I swallowed a mixture of mild panic and exhilaration and made my usual obeisance. 'We'd better get started at once, then.'

'That would be lovely.'

IT IS POSSIBLE THAT when Milady said *take what you need from Stores*, she did not mean *rob the place of everything that might conceivably come in handy, under any circumstances whatsoever.* But if that wasn't what she meant she ought to have particularised, for Jay and I had a daunting job to do and no time at all to do it.

'See, when Milady says "a week",' I said to Jay as I palmed a handy sustenance charm, 'she really means about three days.' I found an unlocking charm — enchanted, unimaginatively, upon a huge bronze key — and pocketed that, too. The Stores at Home are wonderful: half a dozen rooms of varying size, the walls all lined with shelves and cabinets laden with all manner of artefacts, trinkets and Curiosities — and even a few genuine Treasures. Some of them are aged and delicate; you need a special permit to take any of those out. I didn't touch them. I was more than contented with enchantments more recently Wrought, for they offered everything we could need, and one did not have to live in fear of breaking or losing one of them along the way.

'Three days,' murmured Jay. 'Let's see that list again?'

I handed over the slip of paper I'd received from Nell: a computer print-out of all known Troll Enclaves still extant in Britain. The list consisted of twenty-six names, more than half of which she had subsequently crossed out in red pen. Baron Alban's territories, I presumed; we did not need to investigate those. South Moors and Farringale were also crossed off, which left us with nine places to visit.

Nine towns in three days.

Feasible, I hoped, since one of us was a Waymaster. But *damn.* It was going to be intense.

I could see when Jay had finished counting up the names, for his face registered the same dismay as I felt. I quickly took back the list. 'One at a time. That's all we have to think about.'

'Right.' He returned to watching me strip Stores of everything remotely useful, though I felt that his gaze rested more on me than on the surrounding treasures. How did that make sense? New recruits tended to salivate when we brought them in here, and I'd taken Jay straight to the largest of the storerooms. A fabulous late nineteenth-century statue of a mermaid rested on a shelf about three inches from his face, a lovely thing Wrought from jade and something nacreous which visibly rippled with power. A protection charm of some kind was probably embedded therein; it was the kind of thing the wealthy used to like to keep on display in their fabulous houses, to keep thieves and such away.

Jay didn't even glance at it.

'*What?*' I said after a while.

Jay chewed his lip. 'I, uh. Think we may have got off on the wrong foot, just a little.'

Well, he was right. I turned away again to hide my blush, for I *had* messed up. 'I fear I have been patronising, and I apologise. But *really*. If they'd just *told* me that you were—'

'Relevant?' Jay offered.

'Yes. Exactly.' I took down a sweet little teacup painted with viper's bugloss, but regretfully put it back again. I wanted it, but the chances of either of us coming down with a fever in the next three days were not high.

'Apology accepted. But I was speaking more of myself.'

'Oh?'

'I think it was the unicorn symbol, and your...' He trailed off. When I looked back, his gaze was travelling thoughtfully from my wildly-coloured hair, past my madly-coloured dress and all the way down to my whimsically-coloured shoes. He wisely chose not to finish that sentence. 'Ves,' he said instead. 'That's all anybody ever calls you. But you turn out to be *Cordelia Vesper.*'

'Does that name mean something to you?'

He grimaced. 'I read your thesis. "Modern Magick and—"'

'—Magickal Heritage: The Changing Times. I remember.'

'Right.'

I waited, but that seemed to be it. 'Did you...' I paused to reflect, discarding my instinctive question, because *did you like it?* sounded appallingly needy. 'Did you find it... useful?' I hazarded.

'It was interesting.'

Interesting. Right.

I took down one last Curiosity — a floral charm bracelet which, if I knew my charms, purported to change the colour of any bloom I chose to so deface — and stuffed it into my pocket. There was no possible way we could find a use for it, but what did that matter? Life is complicated, and happiness is made up of the little things. I'd bring it back when we got home.

'Shall we go?' I proposed.

'At once, and immediately. Faster than the speed of light. We'll arrive yesterday.'

I blinked. 'Really?'

'Wha— no. No! It was a joke.'

'Oh.' Anything Jay did could only seem sadly mundane after hype like that, but perhaps that was well enough. Who knew what could be going on behind that impassive visage? Maybe Jay suffered from performance anxiety.

AND LO, IT WAS my turn to be ignorant.

Jay led us down into the cellar. This is not a part of the House I have ever had much cause to visit, before. It is mostly used for storage — the boring kind, not relics and artefacts and such — and one or two minor departments I never go to. Our destination therein proved to be a small chamber tucked into one corner, which we reached by way of a lengthy staircase and three winding corridors.

The heavy oak door creaked horribly as Jay coaxed it open.

'Here we are,' said Jay, ushering me inside and closing the door behind me. 'The Waypoint at Home.'

I looked around, unimpressed. The room was barely furnished; naught but a single couch rested against one wall, looking inviting enough with its plump upholstery and overstuffed appearance, but it was not at all elegant. The walls could have used a new coat of paint, or perhaps just a thorough scrubbing; what had probably once been white had dulled to a drab cream. The floor was well enough, but its bare oak boards had not been swept in about a decade either, if I was any judge.

There was nothing else in there, save only for one thing: a ring of nubs of wood, set into the floor. The remains, I judged, of an ancient henge, over the top of which the House had been built.

Clever.

Jay puttered about doing nothing that I could make any sense of, and I waited. I was already beginning to regret my excess of enthusiasm in Stores; the shoulder bag I carried seemed to be growing heavier by the moment. I occupied myself in transferring some of the smaller of its contents into the pockets of my long purple coat, pleased to find that the redistribution helped. A little.

Curse my magpie tendencies.

'So,' I said after a while, when Jay still did not appear to be doing anything productive. 'What happens now?'

'Seriously?'

'Uh... yes?'

'How can you have no idea how a Waymaster works?' Jay was incredulous, which was unfair of him.

'Jay. Nobody knows how a Waymaster works. Our last one left eight and a half years ago to take up a tempting employment offer in Jaipur, and that was the last I saw of her. And she never took me travelling with her anyway.'

'Really?' Jay was silent for a moment. 'What kind of employment opportunity?'

'Jay. Focus.'

'Just how tempting was it?'

'Jay!'

He rolled his eyes, and... a lot happened all at once. He was standing in the middle of the room, and when he raised his arms the air swooped and whirled and gathered itself into a vortex of stars. That is the nicer way I can think of to describe it. If I said it also resembled a twinkly tornado, however, perhaps that better conveys its more alarming qualities.

'Why do people call you Vesper?' he yelled. I still couldn't figure out what he was doing, but it involved some effort, for sweat was forming on his brow. 'Why not Cordelia?'

'I hate my name!'

'It's... it's pretty.'

'Cordelia? Yes! It's a doll name, for pretty, well-behaved girls who take a lot of ballet classes and wear their hair in buns.'

I thought he actually laughed, though that might have been a trick of the light — which was turning awfully peculiar. 'Why not shorten it?'

'To what? Cord? That's a type of string. Dell? That's a magickal reservoir. Or a computer.'

'Ves is unique.'

'Exactly. It—'

I did not make it to the end of this sentence, for with a roar and a *swoop* and a nauseating sensation of the world tilting upside down, we were gone from the Waypoint in the cellar and deposited in an untidy, aching heap somewhere altogether else.

7

JAY LOOKED LIKE HE was strongly disposed to vomit.

'Are you all right?' I said. Quite uselessly, for he clearly was not.

'Fine,' he replied through gritted teeth.

'Your legs are shaking.'

'My everything is shaking. But I'm fine.' He got to his feet and stood, visibly trembling. But since he was also wearing the clenched-jaw look of a man who *will not* be helped, I left him to it and devoted myself to a largely futile attempt to figure out where we had ended up.

We were in the middle of a henge, of course, though it was not the flashy kind that hordes of tourists come to see. Little remained of it but a ring of decaying wooden posts half-sunk in wet earth, and surrounding that (and us) were... trees. Straggly ones, thick enough to obscure whatever lay beyond but otherwise rather sad-looking.

'Place requires some tending,' I said.

'Most of Britain requires some tending.' Jay took a deep breath, stretched, cast a quick glance around himself and set his face resolutely in what appeared to me to be a completely random direction. 'Ready to go?'

'Where? I have no idea where we are.'

'Somewhere in the vicinity of Glenfinnan. We're a few miles away from Finnan Enclave.' He checked my shoes and, oddly, smiled. 'Boots. Good.'

'Why do you seem surprised?'

'I thought you might have shown up in heels or something.'

'I am not that much of an airhead, Mr. Patel.' I haughtily shouldered my bag. 'Lead on.'

Jay's comment did not much surprise me. I am not expected to be much of a walker; you wouldn't anticipate that about a woman with a fondness for delicate, impractical clothes and improbable hair, would you? But actually, I love to walk. I enjoyed our hike, for the environs of Glenfinnan proved to be green hill country, dotted with patches of woodland, and here and there glimpses of an expanse of clear, serene water. The air was bright and crisp and I breathed deeply, somewhat regretful that our errand was of such urgency as to prevent of our exploring.

Jay clearly had no soul for scenery, for he marched on without ever pausing to admire. Nor did he ever waver as to direction. He certainly had focus. He seemed so little inconvenienced by his obvious shakiness before, I didn't want to admit that my knees were shaking, too, and it took half an hour for the waves of nausea to stop assaulting my stomach. I pretended I was fine and so did Jay, and we accomplished our forced-march in rather less than an hour.

Finnan Enclave's front door proved to be at the base of one of those gorgeous, craggy hills, a bit like at South Moors. We stood in the twin shadow of two swelling peaks, one rising on either side of us. Drifty clouds had raced over the sun, and we stood bathed in a mild, unpromising gloom as we studied the green, heathery slopes before us.

'Are you sure this is it?' I said after a while, when Jay seemed undecided.

'Yes.'

All right, then. I waited while Jay rambled about a bit, looking this way and that in a decisive fashion, and occasionally touching protruding rocks.

'Do you know where the door is?' I said at last.

'Of course I do.'

I waited a little longer, watching in idle delight as a tiny pink skreerat poked its head out from in between a tuft of grasses, eyed Jay beadily, and vanished again.

Jay finally gave up his futile search. 'It's one of these,' he said, gesturing broadly at a tumble of fallen boulders.

'How do you know that?'

'I looked them up on Nell's system before we left.'

Clever of him, though it was not currently availing us much. I rummaged in my satchel, ignoring Jay's disbelief as I extracted rather more objects from within than could reasonably fit inside. 'Aha,' I murmured, drawing forth my oversized key and a pendulum, the kind that had probably once belonged inside a grandfather clock. 'This,' I said to Jay, 'is a basic burglar's toolkit, magicker style.' It was the work of a moment to coax the pendulum into activity and it began to swing gently in my hand, back and forth, back and forth. 'It is a little clumsy, the pendulum,' I observed as the charm did its work. 'I would have enchanted a pathfinder's charm onto something a bit more elegant, myself. A filigree compass, for example, with quartz fittings and a handsome chain. But—' I paused as the pendulum's sway slowed and eventually stopped, leaving the device pointing unerringly at a large, craggy black boulder about six feet away from where Jay had stopped. 'It works, proving that elegance is not at all necessary in life.' I smiled, packed the pendulum away again, and advanced upon the boulder.

We had to go through the usual process of requesting entrance, of course. I laid my palm against the boulder and announced us. When that didn't work, Jay tried.

We were not surprised to find that the silent hills remained silent. There was no promising creak of an opening door, no gust of air to welcome us into a yawning portal.

'Breaking and entering it is, then,' I said, with a sense of satisfaction I could not disguise. I can't help it: I love doing things the sneaky way.

Jay was not so thrilled. He did not object, for Milady had essentially *ordered* us to get into these Enclaves one way or another. But he was visibly uncomfortable as I employed my unlocking charm upon the boulder and...

...and nothing. It did not work. Oh, the *key* worked all right; it glimmered with that promising aura of power, and the boulder glittered in response. There was communication between the two charms, as there should have been, but the boulder declined to be affected by it. The rock remained untouched, stubbornly inert and immoveable.

'Some burglar you are,' said Jay.

I put the key away. 'On to Plan C.' That skreer-at had to have come from somewhere. Magickal beasts don't typically wander the wilds as freely as, say, wood mice or stoats or whatever. They mostly stick to the Dells, which are pockets of Hidden landscapes folded between the Ways. Finnan Enclave had firmly closed its outer doors upon the non-magickal world, as they all did, but its regular entrance would undoubtedly be situated on the edge of one of these Dells. If we could not walk straight into the Enclave, we'd have to get into Finnan Dell first and *then* break into the Troll settlement. Their back door, so to speak, was unlikely to be so well protected as their front door.

I went back to the spot where I'd seen the skreerat, and kept walking that way. It wasn't too long before I saw it again: a glimpse of pinkish-grey fur whisking into the concealing cover of a cluster of frondy grasses.

I delved into my satchel again, removed an object which markedly resembled an ordinary torch (because, in essentials, it was), and switched it on. Its beam blazed forth, illuminating the grassy path the skreerat had followed in a haze of misty light.

'Is there anything you aren't carrying in that bag?' said Jay.

'Nope.' I waved the torch around a bit, but the quality of the light did not change.

9

I DO NOT KNOW how Miranda got down to Gloucester so quickly.

It wasn't *that* fast, I suppose; not compared to the (relative) ease with which Jay darts about the country. But she arrived a full hour sooner than I'd expected, and she brought approximately half of the Society with her. Soon, those eerily quiet caverns were awash with frantic Society agents racing to save, protect and preserve as much as they could.

The worst discovery was the crude pit that had been dug at the rear of the Enclave. Its aroma first announced its presence; we lifted our noses to the putrid scent of something rotting, and followed the stench.

It proved to consist of *lots* of somethings rotting. The pit lurked behind a pair of ramshackle, abandoned buildings both leaning dangerously to the left. A narrow track wound in between, and at the rear was the crater: perhaps ten feet deep and eight wide, roughly covered over in tarpaulin in a crude, futile attempt to conceal the horror of its contents. It was a bone pit, and filled nearly to the rim with the half-rotted corpses of dead animals. Most of them had had their flesh roughly stripped from their bones before they were discarded, though by no means expertly. Looking at the mess of bloodied flesh, the pale glint of bone here and there, the thick carpet of maggots crawling with grotesque enthusiasm over the whole, I could imagine the clumsy haste with which each beast had been dispatched to its fate.

They were not all magickal beasts, but too many were. Severed heads and tails and paws, dislocated beaks and feathered crests, claws and teeth, patches of decaying fur — each sad little remnant announced that here lay far too many of the precious creatures we fought so desperately to save.

I wished, too late, that Miranda had been far away when we found that pit. It broke her heart. She stood on the edge of it, shuddering uncontrollably, and looking so near to collapse that I had to steady her.

'How could they?' she gasped. 'How could they do such a thing?'

'Miranda.' I gripped her arm hard, holding her up by sheer force of will if I had to. 'They are sick. Can you understand that? This is not cruelty, it is desperation. They've been eating this much and they are still wasting away. They are *starving*.'

I don't know if she heard me, or registered the import of my words, for she made no reply. She took a deep, deep breath, mopped her damp cheeks on the sleeve of her jumper, and left me. 'Right,' I heard her calling as she walked away. 'There must be some creatures still alive down here, let's find them! Quickly, please!'

Well and good. Miranda's job was to take care of the animals. I needed to find someone who could help the trolls.

They were already being helped, I soon saw as I trotted gratefully away from that terrible pit. But ineptly. The Society had not yet realised how futile it was to try to communicate with the trolls of Darrowdale; we were too late for that. They needed more direct help, though of what nature, who knew?

A young man in a blue jacket raced past on his way to somewhere; I caught hold of him. 'Did they send any of the medical staff down here? I need to talk to them.' I'd asked for a doctor, but requests and instructions sometimes got a little garbled along the way.

'Uh,' said the boy. 'Foster's here somewhere.' He did not stay to argue the point any longer, but dashed off again.

That was all right. They'd sent Rob, and that was all I needed to know. Robert Foster, with all his might, was also a doctor, a fact I sometimes forgot. I went in search of him, but ran into Jay first.

'I was looking for you,' said Jay. 'We're finished at Darrowdale, they can handle it from here. We need to move on.'

'Yes, but first I have to talk to Robert.'

Jay's brow snapped down. 'Can't it wait?'

'No. Help me.'

'Right.' We resumed the search together — a frustrating process, for there were so many people down there, so much furious activity taking place, that it was hard to know where to begin. I saw Miranda once, striding past us with a thunderous look, and Zareen looking unusually grim, but no Robert.

It was Jay who spotted him at last. We had found our way back to that odd little square, where we had met the troll in the suit. Where it had been serene before, it was now swarming with people. 'There,' said Jay, pointing.

Rob was bending over the old lady under her blanket, tending to her with all the gentle care so characteristic of him. He was not trying to speak with her, but examined her face with a look of intense focus.

'Rob,' I said. 'I think there's some kind of a sickness here. They've all got it. Have you been to South Moors?'

Robert straightened up at my words, and directed a frowning look at me. He shook his head. 'Should I?'

'Yes. South Moors is going to end up like this, I know it. They're displaying the same kinds of symptoms, only I think they are at an earlier stage. It's like... some kind of wasting disease, and they're all eating and eating but it's not helping them.'

He nodded thoughtfully, casting an eye over the old lady, who still had not stirred. 'That would make sense with what I am seeing. I'll look into it.'

'There's another thing. The things they are eating — they're mostly going for magickal beasts. Not exclusively, for I saw a fox and a lot of rats in that pit. But either by knowledge or instinct they're targeting the magickals, and that has to be relevant.'

'Thanks, Ves.' He nodded to me and to Jay and turned back to his patient.

'Can we go now?' said Jay.

'Immediately, and at once.'

If I could, I would be delighted to forget the urgent bustle of the next two days. Jay took us across England, into Wales and Ireland and back again;

three great, gigantic, exhausting leaps every day. By the end of it, I was ready to collapse. Jay looked like he wished he had died three weeks ago.

From Darrowdale we proceeded to Parrow Hollow, Warwickshire, which to our relief was hale and well — merely Reclusive. Five of the other names on our list proved much the same, but the final one... that one was as bad as South Moors and Darrowdale put together. Baile Monaidh Enclave was a decimated wreck, well on its way to becoming a ghost town like Glenfinnan. Its handful of surviving citizens were skeletal, withered almost to the point of desiccation, and sunk in such deep stupor they were barely breathing. We summoned all the help we could, but we both knew it was bordering upon too late for them.

By the time we finally made it Home, my trembling legs threatened to dump me face-first into the cold, unforgiving stones of the cellar Waypoint, and I came close to decorating them with a liberal helping of my stomach contents besides. How Jay held himself together I do not know, but somehow he did. As the swirling winds of our passage slowly died away, he stood with his arms tightly folded, jaw clenched, sweat pouring off him.

I eyed him with a view to offering assistance, but he would not meet my gaze.

'I want a bath,' I announced. 'A bath, two meals, three desserts, six cups of tea and sixteen hours in bed.'

Jay made a faint sound that might have been a chuckle, or perhaps it was a choked gasp of pure longing. 'Three meals for me, and make that twenty-four hours asleep.'

'You've earned it.' I hesitated, reluctant to give voice to my next thought. But it couldn't be helped. 'Right after we talk to Milady.'

Jay backed up a step, his eyes widening in horror. 'No! I am not doing that climb!'

'Well...' I forced my jellied legs to walk me to the door, and took hold of the handle. 'This might be one of those times when...' I opened the door and took a peek beyond. 'When House loves us. Look.'

Instead of the narrow, dark passage and staircases of the cellar, the room beyond the door was clearly Milady's tower. 'Just six or seven steps and we're there.'

'Three, if you don't have short legs.' Jay demonstrated one of his long strides, which dwarfed mine. But he never made it to a second. He wobbled and stopped, swaying like a sapling in a strong wind.

'Right, come on.' I took his arm, propped him up against my shoulder, and hauled us both through the door.

Jay promptly collapsed all over Milady's floor. I winced, for he hit the ground with a *thud* and that had to hurt. The carpet might be handsome, but it wasn't especially thick.

The air sparkled.

'Jay Patel,' said Milady. 'Are you well?'

'Fine,' croaked Jay. Probably. It was hard to understand him with his face buried in the rug like that.

Milady let the matter drop. 'Welcome Jay, Ves. You have news for me, I collect.'

'Tons of it.' I gave myself permission to sit, too, if Jay was going to, though I managed the business with a touch more elegance than he. With the help of an occasional, muffled interpolation from Jay, I told Milady everything that had happened since she had sent us off to Glenfinnan.

She heard us out in her customary courteous silence, and then said: 'Very good. There's chocolate in the pot.'

I blinked, taken aback, for I had expected some form of comment upon our labours. A question or two, perhaps; confirmation of a point of detail somewhere; even a titbit of information we might yet be unaware of.

Ah, well. If chocolate was all I could have, chocolate I would most certainly take.

'Do take them back down, House?' said Milady, which surprised me again, for I had never yet heard of anybody directly addressing House and actually receiving a response. But Milady spoke with the confidence of being not only heard but attended to, and so she was, for when we opened the door again we found ourselves stepping over the threshold directly into the first floor common room.

'I like you,' said Jay.

'Thank you.'

'I was talking to the House.'

'I know.'

He gave me a tiny smile, barely more than a twitch of his lips, and sank heavily into the nearest arm chair. The chocolate pot, apparently taking its cues from Milady in the same fashion as House, obligingly poured itself out for both of us, and we disappeared into all the sweet, spicy pleasures of hot chocolate for a blissful two or three minutes.

'Is that it?' said Jay, when he had finished slurping up every last trace of chocolate from his dainty cup.

'Doubtful. Now we wait.'

'For?'

I shrugged. 'Milady does not yet know how to proceed, I would guess. She is most likely awaiting the return of our colleagues from Darrowdale and Baile Monaidh.'

'Why do we have to wait for Milady? Isn't there something we can do in the meantime?'

'Besides sleeping?'

'After the sleeping.'

'Maybe, yes, and I do have an idea. But I want to sleep first. Don't you?'

'Desperately.'

So we did that.

My idea involved a day or two spent searching the libraries; always an appealing prospect, whatever the occasion. But before I had chance to get started, someone swept in upon me and knocked all my plans awry. I was reclining in the common room at the time, stretched across two wing-back chairs and half asleep. It *was* first thing of the following morning, in my defence, and though I had slept a great deal it did not yet feel like enough.

'Vesper?' said a low, beautiful voice, and I jerked upright, for I knew those delectable tones.

Baron Alban was back.

10

AND THERE HE WAS, in all his gorgeous glory. He had chosen a red leather duster coat that day, worn with dark combat trousers, boots to match, and an ivory shirt. No hat; instead, his golden-bronze locks had been brushed into an attractively wind-swept arrangement, and a jewelled pin winked at his throat.

I was suddenly wide awake.

'Hello, the Baron,' I said lightly, wishing I had taken a minute or two longer over my hair before I'd come downstairs. It probably resembled a hedge more nearly than I would like.

The Baron, though, did not seem displeased, for he looked me over with a twinkle and a smile, and made me a bow. 'It is early. I apologise.'

'The pot would like to offer you some tea,' I observed, for the delicate glass teapot I favoured was bobbing lightly up and down, its spout emitting enthusiastic puffs of steam.

'Thank you, pot. I shall be delighted.' He took a seat, and his cup shortly after, and sat looking thoughtfully at me. 'How are you getting along with the matter of the Enclaves?' he said.

I sat up a little more. 'Well, I have a theory, though it has some holes in it. But maybe you can help fill them in.'

He smiled faintly. 'Perhaps I might.'

'I think there is some kind of wasting sickness. They eat and eat and still starve; clearly they are ill. But there has to be more to it than that, because there are too many questions. It *seems* to be affecting only trolls, but why only a few of the Enclaves? And there is no discernible link between those communities that are sick. They are situated far apart from one another, so how is the disease spreading? And they aren't just starving, they are... it's almost like their minds are starving, too. They have no energy for anything but eating, and barely that. They don't speak; it's as if they have forgotten how to form words, or simply lack the energy or the will to make the effort.'

'All good points.'

'And they are eating magickal creatures, almost exclusively. Why? That suggests it is about something more than mere physical sustenance. Any kind of food would suffice there, but they are going for meat, and the meat of magickal beasts in particular. What's that about?'

Alban's green, green eyes twinkled with amusement. 'So many questions. You have some theories to advance, too?'

'Of course I do. But I did not share them with Milady, yet, for I have no evidence.'

'Let's hear them.'

'Right.' I set down my empty tea cup. 'The disease spreads, but if it were contagious in any conventional way, surely we would be seeing either a wider problem — or a more confined one. Some of the affected Enclaves have been at least partially Reclusive for years, with little or no traffic going in or out of their towns. How did they catch it? And since they did, why hasn't it spread farther? I don't think it is a contagion.

'Meanwhile, their desperate need to eat, eat and eat is telling, but the fact that they are starving anyway tells me that whatever they are feeding, it isn't themselves. I think there is some kind of infecting body — a parasite, if you will. And it is taking so much from each host that it's killing them. But it does not need meat to survive.

97

'We know that many magickal beings feed as much off magickal energies as from more conventional foods. Trolls are an example. You need meat, grain, vegetables to survive, but you need a replenishing diet of magickal energies in order to flourish. This is why Troll Enclaves tend to be located inside Dells; those structures as a whole are built around sources of strong magickal energy. It's perfect. At a place like Glenfinnan, you eat, sleep and breathe magick, literally.

'These parasites, then. I think they feed off magickal energy. If we go back to Glenfinnan, say, track down what is, or more probably *was*, their source of magick, I imagine we will find it drained. And that is what happened to its citizens, too. Whatever parasite they were carrying sucked them dry.'

Alban just watched me, his face unreadable, and I began to feel a flicker of doubt. The idea made sense to me, but he did not seem to be impressed. 'Is all of this based purely upon logic and deduction?' he asked.

'Is that not good enough?'

To my relief, he grinned. 'I suspect your theory of such a high level of accuracy, I wondered if you had access to some secret source of information after all.'

'Some secret source of information I ought not to be going anywhere near?' I tried to look coy, as though I might have just such a source.

'Exactly.' The grin faded and a frown appeared, the unsettling kind.

So much for making of myself a woman of mystery. 'Alas, no,' I sighed. '*You* do, of course, but the likes of a Vesper can only dream.'

The grin flashed again, wry this time. 'You are occasionally talked of in my circles, you know. Your track record is impressive — so much so, I think there are those who suspect you of harbouring secret resources. But I begin to think it is merely an astuteness of mind that's hard to hide from.'

'So you *do* have a secret library!'

He laughed. 'Point ably proven.'

'May I see it?'

'Of course not.'

Curses. 'So why are you visiting me this morning?'

'Take a guess.'

'There is something you want me to do.'

'You and your partner, yes. Jay, was it?'

'It is.'

Baron Alban paused, and looked around. The common room was mostly empty at that hour of the morning, but not quite: Miranda sat wearily nursing a coffee on the other side of the room, and another chair was occupied by somebody from the

Restoration department whose name I can never remember. 'Is there somewhere more private we can talk?'

'It's never promising, when they say that in films.'

His lips twitched. 'I have nothing nefarious in mind, I assure you.'

'I don't object to a *little* villainy, mind. I only draw the line at a *lot.*'

This he acknowledged with a gracious salute, and stood up. 'The matter is somewhat urgent.'

'Ohh.' How interesting. I led him out of the common room at once, down to the ground floor and around to the south side. One of my favourite retreats is the expansive conservatory that occupies about half of the south wall. It belongs to the Botany department, and they do a fine job of keeping it filled with all the most interesting magickal herbs and plants, many of which bloom gloriously and smell delicious. I cannot understand why it isn't constantly swarming with people, but I seem to be one of very few who visit if they don't have to.

As I'd hoped, we arrived to find damp stone floors and the scent of wet earth in the air: the watering had already been done for the morning, and we could expect to have a quiet corner of the greenhouse to ourselves for a few minutes. I chose a sunny nook beneath an arching trellis heavy with something blue-blossoming and fragrant, and adopted a posture of intent interest.

The baron was uncharacteristically hesitant. He looked at the flowers, and at me, and at the clear glass ceiling, and appeared to be struggling to discover what to say.

'I need your help,' he finally ventured.

'So you said.'

'On an errand of a... slightly questionable nature.'

'I was getting that feeling, too.'

His eyes smiled at me. 'There is somewhere I urgently need to get into. It relates to the Enclaves, you see, so it is an emergency. But the place in question is locked. *Extremely* locked. And there are one or two other obstacles...' He trailed off.

'If Jay told you I have a taste for breaking and entering, he is quite wrong, and I deny all charges,' I said serenely.

Alban lifted a brow in my general direction. 'He's said nothing of the kind, in fact. *Do* you indeed?'

'As I said, all charges denied.'

'That might not be a bad thing, at all.'

'I grow ever more intrigued.'

Alban sighed. 'Right, the fact is... there are three keys to the place in question. I have secured two of them, at some risk and cost to myself, but they are useless if I can't get all three.'

Uh huh. 'Where is the third one?'

He smiled at me, hope and mischief and sheepishness mixed up into one rather adorable, hard-to-resist package. 'It's, um. It's here.'

'Let me guess: you absolutely are *not* supposed to have it.'

'Let's just say Milady refused.'

It was my turn to raise a questioning brow.

'She threatened to throw me off the tower top,' he admitted.

'Just how locked *is* this place?'

'Extremely, thoroughly, completely and forever locked.'

'I might guess that it is dangerous.'

'Probably. Maybe. Who knows, anymore?'

I folded my arms. 'So. Milady held the prospect of your swift and inescapable death over your head if you pursue this venture and you still want to find the key?'

'No.' His smile broadened, turned achingly hopeful. 'I want *you* to find the key.'

'That is spectacularly unflattering.'

'Depends how you look at it.' He leaned closer to me, so close that I could smell the fresh, cologne scent of him. 'Do I consider you expendable? In no way whatsoever. Do I think you are a match for Milady? Why, yes. I absolutely do.'

My eyes narrowed. 'You cannot flirt me into it, Lord Baron.'

That smile turned wickedly mischievous, and the twinkle reappeared in his eyes. 'Can't I?'

Damn him, he was far too good.

Though, he did not know me perfectly if he thought he *needed* to flirt me into it. I would have done it just for the sake of curiosity alone. A super-locked, mysterious somewhere, filled to the brim with who-knew-*what* manner of juicy secrets? Yes *please.* You can sign me up for that, zero questions asked.

'What is it that you needed Jay for? I possibly don't need to tell you that he will be firmly opposed to this proposition.'

'Quite,' agreed the baron. 'We do not need to tell him about this particular part of it, perhaps, if you think he will disapprove. I will need his Waymastery skills later on, once we have secured the final key.'

'One last question, then.'

He made a show of bracing himself. 'Let's hear it.'

'What, or where, are you trying to get into?'

'I can't tell you that.'

'No good! Try again.'

'Vesper. I can't tell you that.'

'Right. And you were planning to waltz off there with Jay and leave me languishing at Home alone, I suppose?'

He did not answer that in words, but his face told me everything I needed to know.

'You'll tell me, and you'll take me with you.'

'I can't.'

'No deal.'

'Ves... you don't understand.'

'And I never will, if you keep me in the dark.'

He sighed, ran a hand over his hair — unwise, for those wavy locks were *so* perfectly ordered before, and what a shame — and eyed me with strong disfavour. 'I could find someone else to get hold of the key.'

'If there is a better choice, why are you talking to me?'

'Fine.' He made a don't-blame-me-when-you're-dead gesture and said, with strong reluctance: 'Where we are going, if you really want to know—'

'I do.'

'—Is... is Farringale.'

11

'Farringale,' I repeated.

'Yes,' said Baron Alban.

'Mythical, mysteriously abandoned, long-lost seat of the Troll Court for hundreds of years Far-ringale?'

'That's the one.'

'The unfindable version, or is there some other Farringale that's still marked on a map somewhere?'

'Why don't you let me worry about how to find it, while you worry about how to get in?'

'All right. Be right back.' I slid past him and made for the door.

'Uh, Ves?' he called. 'Where are you going?'

'I'm going to ask Milady.'

'What? Why! She will only say no.'

'You don't know that for sure.'

'No,' said Milady.

I'd given it my best shot, honest. I had begun with a polite enquiry after her health, paired with my usual curtsey, and opened the discussion with: 'It emerges that our excellent Baron Ambassador suspects a close connection between the afflicted Enclaves and Farr—'

'No,' said Milady.

'—Farringale, and seeks an opportunity to investigate the precise causes of its demise in a more direct fashion—'

'No.'

'—in hopes of uncovering some new, hitherto unsuspected information which might enable us to save Baile Monaidh and Darrowdale and—'

'No.'

'—any others that might come under similar afflictions in the future, or even to—'

'No!'

'—to learn enough to avert such calamities from ever occurring again at all. '

'Vesper! I do not know how many times you require me to repeat the same word before you find yourself able to comprehend it.'

'But why! The Baron's theory is sound and his cause is more than just—'

'The reasons he saw fit to present to you, and to me, are just, but I suspect the Baron of harbouring a few other ideas.'

'If he draws some other benefit out of the venture while also resolving an *emergency* which threatens the life of many of his people, I see no cause for complaint.'

'His theory might be sound, or it might be hogwash. There are reasons aplenty to avoid Farringale. Why do you think it was closed in the first place?'

'If it *is* sound, much may be accomplished. If it is not, we will have learned something.'

'And the risks?'

'Baron Alban is prepared to face them, and he has already secured two keys—'

'The keepers of those keys cannot have been any more delighted with this plan than I am, so I am moved to question just by what means his lordship secured them.'

'That is his own affair. I did not ask.'

Milady sighed, its manifestation a soft *puff* of glittering light. 'Vesper. I understand your point of view, truly, and I applaud your passion. But consider. The risks involved in opening Farringale are not necessarily limited to those holding the keys. We do not know *what* may come forth, were those doors opened, and therefore we cannot consider ourselves prepared to deal with the consequences.'

'The only way to learn something is to ask! To explore, to find out! No secret ever did anybody any good for long.'

'Vesper.' Milady's tone turned less strident, more... resigned. Wearily so. 'I cannot permit this.'

'I can only continue to fervently disagree with that decision.'

'You are one of my very best, and you know it. But I hope you understand that your job will be in some considerable danger, should you choose to disobey me in this.'

'I understand.'

'Very good. Please accept my regrets, Ves.'

I DID, OF COURSE, with the utmost politeness. But while I understood Milady's position well enough, I do not think she understood that keeping my job was not my primary priority. Oh, I would be devastated if she carried through her threat, and ejected me from the Society. It has been my home and my world for so long, I cannot imagine my life without it. But it is a job with a *purpose*. The work that I

I thought about all the obvious places, and dismissed them as too obvious. The tower? On the one hand, at least she could keep an eye on it up there. No one was likely to be pilfering it out from under her very eyes. But it did not strike me as likely, because whenever any of us thinks of Milady, we think of the tower. It is the first place any of us would choose to look for something Milady had hidden, and therefore, I had to cross it off the list. She was too subtle for that.

Stores? That made a lot more sense to me, and I considered it an attractive possibility for a while. Where better to hide something like that than in plain sight, so to speak? Buried under so much other, random paraphernalia that nobody would ever realise its importance? Maybe. But this, too, occurred to me too early and too easily, so I had to discount it. Anything that seemed very likely probably wasn't.

I thought about the Enchanting labs for similar reasons. They spend all day tinkering with various charms and imbuing them into various objects, so those labs are always littered with stuff — keys included. But that struck me as too random. Such a key could get lost in there, or worse yet, its operating charm overwritten with something else entirely. Milady wouldn't be that careless.

And so I went on, eliminating every idea I came up with as too obvious, too unlikely, or too risky, until I had nothing left.

I toyed briefly with the idea of asking Jay. I'm not sure why, only that he was bright-minded and obviously saw the world very differently from me. He would probably see some possibility that would never have occurred to me. But I kept coming back to the unavoidable fact that he would heartily disapprove of the whole venture, so I stayed away from him.

In the end, devoid of further ideas, I went to see Valerie.

VALERIE GREENE HAS A job I rather envy. She's Queen of the Library, Head of History, Boss of all Secrets, and it is her official duty to uncover exactly the kinds of ancient mysteries that I cannot resist. I applied to join the Library Division when I arrived at the Society, but Milady said my varied talents rendered me better suited to my current, rather more eclectic role, and I cannot say that she was wrong there.

Nonetheless, when I walk into the grand library at Home and see Valerie at the main desk there, absorbed in some promisingly huge and dusty tome and with her name engraved upon a shiny brass plaque, I always suffer a mild stab of regret. It is one of those libraries that dreams are made of: all soaring ceilings and shelves by the thousand, everything all ancient oak wood and leather-bound tomes. It smells like knowledge and mystery and time, and when I went in that day I paused to take a great lungful of that familiar aroma, as I always do.

Valerie looked up from her book. 'Morning, Ves.' She had a smile for me, as usual. She is one of the few people at Home that I would call a close friend; we've both been here for years, and have spent many hours chattering about books and speculating as to the truth behind some mystery or another. She and I are roughly the same age, she being the elder by only a few years. She has a neatness and a chic style about her that I have never been able to match, her dark hair and skin always perfectly complemented by her ensemble. She favours the swept-up look by way of hairstyle, which is practical; when I read, my hair is always falling all over the pages. You would think I would learn.

'Val.' I sidled up to the desk — a mildly undignified form of movement it may be, but it cannot be helped; sidling is exactly what I did — and sat down across from her. 'I need to ask you something.'

'Is this going to be one of those juicy requests?'

'It is the questionable kind. Is that juicy enough?'

'Plenty.' She closed her book with great care and set it aside, laying it atop a soft, protective cushion. 'What are we digging up today?'

I grinned. Val knows me far too well. 'A key,' I said. 'Actually, before we get to the sticky part, let's begin with Farringale. What do you know of it?'

That word definitely got her attention. 'Farringale? Much the same things everybody knows about it, I imagine. Seat of Their Gracious Majesties, the kings and queens of the Troll Court since time immemorial, up until a few centuries ago. Its last known rulers were Hrruna the Third and Torvaston the Second, whose reign ended somewhere in the mid sixteen hundreds but who knows when exactly, because it—'

'—inexplicably faded out of all knowledge. Exactly. That's the part that I'm interested in.'

Valerie folded her arms and gave me the narrow-eyed look. 'Theories abound as to why, as I am sure you know, because you have read every book we own about Farringale from cover to cover. So why are you asking me?'

'I might be under the impression that you know something that isn't in any of those books.'

'I wish I did, but no. The current Court keeps that place shrouded in the kind of secrecy that can only be termed impenetrable.'

I nodded, more impressed than I cared to show. Valerie is tenacious with this kind of thing, even more so than I am, and she has the stature and credentials to make legitimate requests for that level of information. If even she couldn't get past the Troll Court, they were really serious about keeping it under wraps.

'Somebody at the Court disagrees,' I said, and I told her about Baron Alban and his proposition. Her eyes grew rather wide as I hurried through my tale, and when I had finished she said: 'Ves, I don't know whether you should... are you sure about this?'

'Of course I'm sure,' I replied, all incredulity.

And then came the grin I had expected. 'Of course you are. As if I would make any other decision in your shoes.'

'I wouldn't suspect you of it for an instant.'

12

'SO YOU NEED THIS key.' Valerie tapped a pen thought-fully against her lips, a characteristic gesture. I said nothing, letting her think in peace. I have great confidence in Val. She always comes up with some-thing. 'I wonder why Milady has custody of it,' she said at length.

A good question, one I had not really considered. 'The Society's entire existence is about protecting rare old stuff, isn't it?'

'Might be reason enough.' She thought some more, her eyes straying to the books on the far shelves. 'The House predates Milady by quite a margin, of course. I wonder why Alban is so certain Milady is keeping the key.'

A faint suspicion entered my head. 'Predates? By how far?'

She nodded, following my train of thought perfectly — or perhaps I was following hers. 'The House's precise date of construction is not known for some reason, but a few particular architectural features have led me to conclude that it was built somewhere around the early 1660s. Give or take a few years.'

'And the decline of Farringale took place in 1657! Or so Milady said.'

Val's eyes narrowed. 'That was unusually forthcoming of her.'

'Wasn't it? I have no idea what came over her.'

'It makes sense that those three keys were hidden away sometime fairly soon after the close of the Enclave, which was probably somewhere in the 1660s. Is Milady personally keeping the third key, or was it given to the House?'

'Given... to the House?' I was sceptical, I couldn't help it. 'Come on, Val. I know it's an odd House and rather more aware than most Houses are, but still. It doesn't have a mind, exactly, or a consciousness the way we do—'

'Doesn't it?'

It might have been a coincidence, but something creaked in the library just then. I don't mind admitting that it gave me the chills. 'All right,' I said, prepared to accept the possibility, for what was ever normal about the Society? 'But if House has got it, that's a problem. If I couldn't persuade Milady to let me have it, I... have no idea how to convince a seventeenth-century country mansion.'

Valerie smiled. 'House can be very helpful, if it likes you.'

I cast a slightly trepid glance at the stately shelves nearby, and the graceful ceiling arching far over-head. 'How do I know if it likes me?' I whispered.

'I wouldn't worry, Ves. You are very likeable.'

'That's comforting.'

She sat back, eyeing me speculatively. 'I will tell you a secret about the House. Maybe it will help.'

I blinked. 'Wait. There are secrets about the House that you haven't told me?'

'Yes, but we can wrangle about that later. Is this urgent or not?'

'Sorry.'

Out came the secret. 'House has a favourite room. Few have seen it, for it is so well hidden, you really have to know that it's there in order to find it at all. And I don't think House likes visitors in there too often, so it doesn't exactly help you out if you go looking for it. But it's there, somewhere near the heart of the building. A sitting room, prettily decorated, and as far as I can tell it's unchanged since the sixteen hundreds. I believe it most likely belonged to whoever built this House, and House keeps it just the way it is.'

'Fantastic,' I breathed. 'So you've been inside it?'

'Twice.' She did not elaborate, and I didn't push. 'Anyway, if you go there, I think House might listen to you. And if it does... well, House and Milady are usually in accord with one another, but it wouldn't be the first time they have disagreed.'

'Dear Val, you are a jewel in the Society's crown.'

She smirked. 'I know. Got some paper? The directions are a little convoluted, you'll want them written down.'

SHE WASN'T KIDDING. I left the library a few minutes later with a sheet of notepaper in my hand, both sides of it mostly covered in Val's flowing handwriting. According to the directions, there were at least three times as many staircases at Home than I had ever seen or imagined, and far more corridors than the place should reasonably have room for. Not that this should have surprised me either. I had more than once suspected that the House was somewhat larger on the inside than its exterior would lead a person to expect.

Val's route started, helpfully, from the library, but I soon began to feel that I was lost. I trotted along several winding corridors, up a few twisting stair-cases and down several more. At first I knew exactly where I was, but after a while I realised I recognised nothing that I saw around me. When I opened an occasional door to take a peek inside, I saw rooms I had never seen before either.

This frankly flabbergasted me. I had lived for more than a decade in that House, and I'd been comfortable that I knew it inside out. How could so much of it have been hidden from me all that time? And what else was there that I still did not know about?

It grew quieter as I walked, a clear sign that I was travelling farther and farther away from the House's centres of activity. There was a stillness to the air that made me feel very alone, and my footsteps rang out, crisp and sharp, echoing off the aged stonework.

And then the corridor ended. I turned a cor-ner and saw before me nothing but uninterrupted stone walls and a clean stone floor — curiously free of dust and debris, for all its remote atmosphere. There were no windows, no doors, no stairs; no way out at all, except back the way I had come.

I consulted Val's directions again, to no particular avail. Honestly, the sense of giving a woman like me so complex a list of directions and expecting me to traverse them without getting lost! For an instant I suspected Val of playing a trick on me, but dismissed the idea. She would not. Her faith in my ability to find my way through this maze of a castle must be rather higher than my own.

Turn left, said the last of Val's notes, which I had just done. Turn left... and then what? I considered calling her to ask, but dismissed that idea, too. She hates to have ringing phones around when she's reading, and would undoubtedly have switched hers off.

I felt my way along the walls for a while, checking for hidden doors, stones that might obligingly slide aside to reveal secret staircases, that kind of thing. No luck there either.

I chose a corner at the end of the corridor and sat down with my back against the stone wall, surveying the empty passageway before me with some dismay. How could I be *so* inept? The answer was probably obvious, so obvious that it had not occurred to Val that I might need help. Jay would have got it in an instant, and treated my confusion with that faint but distinct disbelief I have sometimes detected in his eyes. I could have called him, but my pride revolted against that idea.

'Well, House,' I said aloud as I hauled myself back to my feet. 'Your secrets are safe from me.' I walked back along that puzzling corridor and turned right, following Valerie's directions backwards.

Memory is a strange thing, is it not? I remember names, dates, faces and all manner of minute details with the greatest of ease, but I am not so well able to recognise places I have already been. So it took me much longer than it should have to realise that the passageway I was walking down was not the same one I had traversed perhaps half an hour before. The great stone blocks that made up the walls were limestone of a slightly different shade, and cut a little on the smaller side. The air smelled faintly of chocolate, which I had not noticed before. When I passed a gilt-framed painting of an eighteenth-century landscape I did not remember seeing before, I was certain I had gone wrong.

My stomach fluttered with nerves at finding myself so much at a loss, for I had clearly strayed from Val's directions and had no idea where I was. If I became hopelessly turned about in House's twisting corridors, would it consent to rescue me? I could be lost for hours. Days.

But then there was a door. It obtruded itself upon my notice so suddenly as to arouse my suspicions. Had it been there a moment before? Was I so oblivious as to have missed it? It looked innocuous enough: an ordinary-sized door painted bright white, with a single, large pewter knob set into the centre.

'All right, then,' I muttered, game to try anything that might get me out of that mess of a maze. I grasped the knob, finding it strangely warm under my hand, and turned it.

And there it was: House's favourite room. It could only be that, for before me lay a perfectly preserved parlour whose fittings and furniture clearly proclaimed its provenance. The wallpaper was prettily figured with scrolling flowers, all rosy and lavender and ivory in hue; three elegantly-curved seventeenth-century chairs had been upholstered to match, in handsome ivory silk; portraits in oval frames hung upon the walls, and an exquisite old grandfather clock occupied one corner. It was still ticking, its pendulum keeping time with a drowsy, soothing sway.

A little white tea table stood in the centre, atop which sat a silver chocolate pot not wholly unlike Milady's. A puff of steam drifted from its spout as I stepped over the threshold, and a cup appeared beside it.

'Is that for me?' I said.

The pot puffed steam again, which seemed a clear enough response. So I settled into the nearest chair — carefully, carefully; one is used to treating antique furniture with great care. But these chairs, while they had obviously been much used and loved, displayed none of the frailty or decay they ought to have accumulated over the better part of four hundred years.

I took a moment to examine the portraits, idly curious as to whether I might recognise any of the faces depicted therein. I did not. They were ladies and gentlemen for the most part, sumptuously garbed in the silk and lace gowns, the elaborately curled wigs, the velvet coats and jewelled extravagance of the sixteen hundreds. There were one or two exceptions, however. I saw a young, dark-skinned man clad in much simpler garb, his expression earnest and intense. On the other side of the room, a little girl in a plain dress played with a doll; next to her portrait hung that of an elderly woman wearing an eighteen-thirties day dress and a wide straw bonnet, smiling in the sunlight of a bright spring day.

'Dear House,' I began, setting down my empty cup. 'Thank you for the chocolate, you are always such a gent. Or a lady, it's... hard to tell. I have come to entreat your help. May we talk?'

It felt odd, sitting alone in that eerie little parlour out of time, literally talking to the walls. But a faint *creak* of assent answered my question to the apparently empty air — or at least, I took it as assenting. Nothing leapt out to cut me off, or to hustle me out of the room again. And so I began.

13

'DEAR HOUSE,' I SAID. Only as I spoke those words did it strike me as odd that the house had no other name. Such grand places always have spectacular names of course — think of Chatsworth, or Castle Howard, or Buckingham Palace. Iconic buildings, memorable names. Why was this one so different? Had it ever been named, at all? If not, why not?

I had never heard of its ever being called anything but "House", or "Home", or something along those lines. It had never felt strange to call it such before. But now I was addressing the building directly, and it felt as strange to call it "House" as it would be to address a friend as "Person", or perhaps "Human".

'Dear House,' I said again, trying to sound less doubtful about it. 'I... need your help.'

I paused — to collect my thoughts, and to give House an opportunity to turf me out, if it wanted to. I mean, if it was going to be totally uninterested in rendering me any assistance at all, better to know that right away and save both of us the time.

But nothing happened, so I went on. 'There is a problem with the trolls, you see. They are sick, dying. We're going to lose a few of their Enclaves altogether if we don't figure out why, and who knows where it will end? Perhaps they will all go. Something has to be done, but nobody knows where to *start.*

'We think it might have something to do with Farringale. Baron Alban and I, that is — do you know him? He is the Troll Court's ambassador to the Hidden Ministry, and he knows things about the Old Court, even if he won't confide in me. We want to go to Farringale, so we can try to find out what destroyed it. If it's the same thing that's wiping out Glenfinnan and Darrowdale and Baile Monaidh, well, maybe we will be able to do something about it. *Before* any more are lost.'

I took a deep breath, encouraged by the continued lack of dire consequences to my narration. 'You've probably guessed why I'm here by now. Alban has two of the keys, but we cannot go without the third. I... may as well own that Milady forbids the venture entirely. I don't really blame her, either.

If Farringale was half as vast and splendid as the legends say, then whatever destroyed it was probably not something we want to poke with a stick. But I think we have to try.

'Val thought you might help me, and... I am hoping she is right. Do you have the third key? Will you lend it to me? I promise to bring it back.' An unpleasant thought entered my head and I felt obliged to add, in a lower tone, 'Assuming I get out of Farringale alive.'

Silence. Seconds passed, then minutes, and I heard no sound but the gentle ticking of the grandfather clock; saw nothing move, save the clock's swaying pendulum.

Was that a refusal? Was the House even listening to me? I didn't know, couldn't tell. All I could do was wait, which I did with increasing impatience and dismay as minute after minute passed and the chocolate went cold in the pot.

Five minutes. Seven. Ten.

Fifteen.

How was I going to explain to Baron Alban that I had failed? He had asked me specifically, with a flattering confidence in my ability to deliver. I did not want to disappoint him. And if we could not get into Farringale, how else were we to save the Enclaves? What else could we do?

Twenty minutes, and no sign of a response. Either House had not heard me at all, or it had chosen to side with Milady. 'Very well, then,' I said. 'Thank you for listening to me. And for letting me see your favourite room.' I took a last look around, for the chances were that I would never see it again.

The clock ticked on.

I hauled myself out of the chair — really, they were surprisingly comfortable, for all their formal magnificence — and shook out my hair.

Something fell from my lap with a *clink.*

Ohgod. Was it my cup? Had I left that dainty and probably priceless antique upon my knee? But no; there had been no shatter, no *crash* of porcelain breaking into pieces.

A key lay upon the floor, not three inches from my left foot. It was a large, handsome, silver-wrought thing, intricately engraved, and it bore a blue jewel that glittered with its own light.

'Oh.' I bent to pick it up, carefully, as though it might be fragile. But it was heavy in my grasp, sturdy, and faintly warm to the touch. That jewel shone when my fingers touched it, mesmerising.

'Thank you,' I whispered. This was no small thing. House was trusting my judgement over Milady's — mine and Alban's. 'We won't fail,' I said, so rashly, for I had no idea what we might find in Farringale; how could I be sure that we would not?

My show of confidence pleased the House, though, for a ripple of warm air shivered over my skin like a balmy summer breeze, and the key glimmered on in my hand.

'Onward, then,' said I, and left the parlour. When I stepped over the threshold of the door, I found myself back in the first floor common room.

And there was Jay, lounging in an arm chair not three feet away and looking at me like I had just grown a second head. 'Where did you spring from?'

I glanced about, confused. 'I came in through a door... oh.' The door was on the other side of the room, and I was nowhere near a window.

'You walked out of a wall,' said Jay.

'Doesn't seem unlikely.' Happily, nobody else was around to witness my involuntary feat of defiance of all known laws of nature, if not Magick; the common room was empty besides him. I wandered over to my favourite chair — the wing-back one with the red upholstery — and flopped down into it with a spectacular lack of grace. I was feeling a bit weak at the knees, which was probably a sign of incipient panic. What did I think I was doing, proposing to waltz into Farringale? A place nobody had set foot inside in centuries, which had collapsed due to reasons unknown but undoubtedly dire? I was mad. Baron Alban was mad.

And the next thing I had to do was convince Jay to get us there, the same Jay who was scowling at me with that fierce frown of his.

'Are you okay?' he said abruptly.

'What?'

'Are you all right? You look a little pale.'

'I am always a little pale.'

He rolled his eyes. 'Paler than usual. You look like a bowl of yoghurt.'

'I'm fine.' The question discomfited me, because it was unexpected. From his face, I'd assumed he was displeased with me for some reason. Instead, he had shown concern.

It did make it harder to proceed to knowingly pissing him off.

Oh well. Delaying unpleasant duties never made them any easier to perform. 'Jay, I need your help with something.'

He sat up a bit, and focused a more alert gaze upon me. 'That is why I am here.'

'It isn't exactly why you— oh, never mind. I need to go somewhere quickly, together with... someone else.'

'Someone who else?'

'Baron Alban.'

He nodded, unconcerned. So far, so good. 'Where are we going?'

'I don't... know, exactly, but Alban does.'

The frown reappeared. 'We are following the intriguing baron into parts wholly unknown? Are we trusting him enough for that? He's a total stranger.'

'It isn't... *entirely* unknown. I know where we are aiming for, I just don't know where it *is*.'

'Enough mystery, Ves. What's going on?'

So much for breaking it to him gently. 'We are going to Farringale.'

'Farri— the Troll Court? The lost one? Seriously?'

'That's the plan.'

He stared at me.

I stared back.

If I had harboured any hopes that he might assume Milady had given the order, those hopes were swiftly dashed. 'Why,' said he with detestable and inconvenient astuteness, 'is it you asking me about this? Why aren't we up in the tower hearing all about it from Milady, together?'

'Because she said no.' Screw trying to be subtle, if he was going to be so bloody clever.

'Then we aren't going.' Jay said this with aggravating serenity, picked up the book he'd been reading when I came in, and to all appearances forgot my existence altogether.

'We are. Look.' I fished the key out of the pocket I'd hastily stuffed it into, and held it up. The blue jewel blazed, which made for quite the impressive effect.

Jay didn't even look up.

'*Jay.* Look at this thing!'

He raised his head, and subjected the glittering key to a dull, uninterested stare. 'What of it?'

'It's the key to Farringale. The third key, of three. House gave it to me.'

'The House gave it to you?'

'Yes.'

'This House?'

'*Yes.*'

And I'd got him, I could see that. He still did not like the idea, but he was listening to me. 'Why would House give you that key if Milady said no?'

'Apparently it isn't up to Milady to decide about the key.'

Jay put away the book. 'All right. Why did Milady say no, if House is in favour?'

'She thinks it's too dangerous to open Farringale.'

'She could well be right.'

'She might be, but so what? How else are we going to help the Enclaves? Do you have a better idea?'

'There are probably hundreds of other ways we could find out what's going on with those Enclaves.'

'Probably. Name one.'

He opened his mouth, hesitated. 'The... the library probably has some relevant materials somewhere, or some other library.'

'That could take forever to dig up.'

'There are teams at Darrowdale and South Moors right now, looking for a source of the trouble—'

'Which they apparently aren't finding in a hurry, as we've heard nothing. And this is urgent, Jay.'

'I am not sure why you expect to walk into Farringale and have the answer handed to you on a plate.'

'I don't, but we *might*. How do you know?'

'You could die. *We* could die.'

'Maybe. Maybe not. Meanwhile, a lot of trolls *are* dying.'

Jay began to look a little desperate. 'Ves... you might be able to openly disobey Milady, but I can't. You've a ten-year history with the Society, a blazing track record. However angry Milady might be with you, the chances of her chucking you out are practically zero. But me? I've only just got here!'

'You're a Waymaster, the only one we've managed to get hold of in about a decade. She won't discard you lightly.'

'It would be neither wise nor classy to presume upon that.'

'House is in favour!'

'Which is useful to know, but House doesn't pay my salary, and House isn't going to be writing me a reference if I have to go looking for a new job.'

'You're a Waymaster, you don't need a reference. You could walk into a new job this afternoon.'

'It's about professional standards, pride—'

'Jay, the important thing here is to get the job done. And the job is to preserve. The Enclaves are folding around us and nobody knows how to stop it. This is the best way I can think of to find out why — the best, the most direct, hopefully the fastest. Can you think of a better one? Really?'

Jay sighed, long and deeply, and shook his head. 'Nope.'

'Right.'

'Right. So.' He scowled at me and chucked his book at my head. 'Damn you and your rule-breaking ways. You'll make a disgrace of me.'

'Or a hero.'

'Or a hero.' He stood up, stretched, shook himself, as if to shake away his doubts. 'Since this is all kinds of urgent, I imagine you want to get going. Where's Alban?'

'I'll find out.' I took out my phone and called the baron's number. His reply was immediate.

'Ves? Did you get the key?'

'Yes.'

'Is Jay with us?'

'Yes.'

'Then we go. Meet me in the conservatory in five minutes.'

'Ten,' I countered. 'We need to grab a few things first.'

'Ten it is.'

14

THE THINGS I HAD in mind were not supplies, as the baron probably imagined. I still had my stash of toys from the Darrowdale expedition, and I keep a basic travel kit ready at all times because I am often sent off somewhere at a moment's notice.

No, the "things" I planned to grab in passing consisted of just the one, really. A tall, reassuringly bulky, Rob-Foster-shaped thing, to be precise.

I like Rob so much. He is so calm, and so obliging. I found him in the infirmary tending to a forlorn-looking soul with her arm in a cast. Broken bones aren't too uncommon around here, at least among those following certain fields of specialisation (mine included).

'Much as I hate to disturb you,' I said to Rob as I swept in, resembling, most likely, a small, vibrant-ly-coloured whirlwind, 'I have an urgent matter on hand.'

Rob acknowledged my appearance but did not answer me until he had finished whatever he was doing for the girl — I call her such because she *was* very young, perhaps fifteen or so. She seemed a bit too young for a Society recruit, but perhaps she was here on some kind of internship or work experience thing. We sometimes get them.

Anyway, Rob dismissed her, all calm reassurance and comforting professionalism, and the girl — Indian, at a guess, and very smartly dressed — went away looking less forlorn.

'All right, Ves,' said Rob, taking off his doctor's coat. 'What may I do for you?'

'Jay and I are going to Farringale,' I told him.

'Ah.'

Unflappable, Rob. 'Nobody's been there in centuries,' I added.

'Indeed.'

'Since we have no idea what we might find there, and whether or not it will prove to be friendly, I'd like to take you along with us.'

Rob looked curiously at me. 'What do you need me for?'

'I'd like your help with not dying.'

He smiled faint amusement. 'Playing the damsel? You could probably hold your own against pretty much anything, and Jay's no slouch either.'

He wasn't wrong — about me, at least; I had no real idea what Jay's abilities might be. Anybody taking up my line of work with the Society is obliged to take a rigorous series of courses in what Milady, by way of adorable euphemism, terms "the Direct Arts". And while I am no prodigy by any means, I can be plenty *direct* when I need to be. I'm still breathing, aren't I? And believe me, Milady has thrown me at all manner of risky adventures down the years.

However.

'It's the "probably" part that bothers me,' I answered. 'And I'll have Jay with me. He is something of a protege and I do not want to have to admit to Milady that I got him sliced up and made into mincemeat.' Particularly when the mission was unauthorised in the first place.

'I'm surprised Milady didn't think of sending me along,' said Rob, brows slightly raised in mild enquiry.

People are too sharp around here by half. 'She doesn't know we're going,' I told him. I mean, why bother lying? 'Actually, she outright forbade it. But House disagrees, so we're going anyway.'

Rob absorbed this in stoic silence, his gaze on me thoughtful. 'All right,' he said, to my relief. 'You can explain the rest on the way.'

I gave him my best, absolutely my sunniest smile, and my most exquisite curtsey too. 'You are a gentleman above any other, Mr. Foster.'

'I know.'

IT WAS ONLY ONCE we arrived at the conservatory that I realised I'd forgotten to mention Baron Alban to Rob. And I had, of course, neglected to mention Rob to Baron Alban. Oops.

The two gentleman took the surprise well, however, electing only to eye one another up in a manner assessing and wary but in no way hostile.

'Our party's expanding,' noted the baron.

'I like breathing,' I told him. 'And Rob's the best we have at keeping all those kinds of procedures going. In numerous ways.'

Alban accepted this with a nod. Rob asked no questions at all, so I left the problem of explaining the Baron's presence for later.

'The key?' prompted Alban.

I fished it out of my pocket and held it up. Rob stared at it with more interest than he had yet shown in anything, that I could remember, but he made no move either to touch it or to ask me about it.

Baron Alban, however, did both.

'No,' I said, snatching it out of his reach. 'I will hang onto this one.'

Alban's eyes narrowed. 'I have the other two.'

'Which you are welcome to keep. House gave this one into my care, however, and I promised to give it back.'

'And so you shall, once we return.'

I shook my head, and tucked the key away again safely out of sight. 'I live here, and I'd like to continue to do so for a while yet. Would you like to break a promise to a castle, voluntarily or otherwise?'

The twinkle returned to the baron's eyes, and he made no further effort to persuade me. 'Where did you find it?'

'That's a secret.'

He rolled his eyes. 'You people eat, sleep and breathe secrets.'

'Pot, meet kettle.'

'Fair.'

Jay arrived just then, looking a little out of breath. I wondered what he had been doing with himself for the last quarter-hour. 'The Waypoint's ready,'

143

he said. He looked at the baron. 'Where are we heading for?'

'I'll tell you when we get to the Waypoint.'

Jay shrugged and turned away. 'Let's go, then.'

A few minutes later we were back in that cold cellar room. It was even colder than last time, and I shivered. Did I imagine the faint, chill breeze coiling sluggishly over the stone floor?

Jay shepherded the three of us into the centre of the floor, right where the winds of travel had manifested last time. Then he looked questioningly at the baron.

'Winchester,' said Alban. 'Or thereabouts.'

Winchester? As far as I had ever heard, scholars were agreed upon just one point regarding Far-ringale: it lay somewhere in the far north, either in England or in Scotland.

Winchester is in Hampshire. In fact, it is almost as far south as you can go before you hit saltwater. How could so many fine minds be so spectacularly wrong, and about so basic a fact?

Pot, meet kettle. Indeed. 'Misdirection?' I said to Baron Alban, failing to conceal my sourness.

He grinned at me. 'Best way to keep a secret I know.'

'You all have been mighty determined to keep this one.'

144

He shrugged. 'Not my call, but I'm sure their Majesties have their reasons.'

'They aren't going to be pleased with you.'

'About as pleased as Milady's going to be with you, I imagine.'

There was time for no more words, for the breeze became a strong wind and then a howling gale, and then *away* we were once again.

Winchester made some sense, I thought, and it was a thought I clung to as I was whirled about, doll-like, in the winds of Jay's magick on the way to Hampshire. After all, while ancient England cannot be said to have had a fixed capital in the modern way, Winchester was its principal city before London supplanted it. It did not surprise me greatly that the Troll Court should choose to anchor itself in the same environs as the monarchs of England, though that did not answer the question of why either party had chosen Winchester in the first place. What was it about the city? It was one of the very oldest settlements in England, true, but the same could be said for many another place.

Such reflections carried me through the worst of the journey, until I was at last set down — surprisingly gently — atop a wide, green hill in some pleasingly sun-dappled countryside. Vibrant meadowland stretched before me, dotted with yellow-flowering bushes and low, dark green shrubs. A brisk wind blew up on the heights there, which would have pleased me more if I had not just been subjected to rather an excess thereof.

I cast a quick glance at Baron Alban, who looked unaffected. Interesting. Did they have a Waymaster at the Troll Court? Most likely. He had the serene air of a man well used to travelling by high winds.

Rob, I knew, was considerably less accustomed to it, but he stood admiring the scenery with his customary stoicism, so I felt no concern for him.

Jay was another matter. I swiftly concluded that it must be much harder to convey four people to the other end of the country than it was to convey two, for he had collapsed into a boneless heap upon the grass and was performing a creditable impression of a dead person.

When a couple of minutes went by and Jay did not get up, Rob knelt beside him and subjected him to a cursory examination. 'You all right, lad?' he said quietly.

'Be fine,' Jay mumbled.

Rob did not argue with this announcement, but took a charm bead out of a pocket somewhere and put it between Jay's lips. They tend to be colour-coded; this one was yellow, and as far as I could remember that meant it was a restorative.

A most effective one, for Jay was soon sitting up and then back on his feet, shaking himself like a dog and breathing great gulps of air. 'Ouch,' he croaked after a while.

Rob clapped him on the shoulder. 'How long have you been using the Ways?'

'About five minutes, as these things go.'

'You did well.'

Jay said nothing in reply, but he accepted the praise with an air of quiet gratitude of which I took careful note. It hadn't occurred to me that he might lack confidence, or that a simple compliment would go such a long way.

'To Winchester, then?' said Jay, looking at Baron Alban.

'Actually, to Alresford.'

That won him a blank look. 'Where?'

'It is a tiny old town a ways north-east of Winchester.'

Jay tapped away at his phone for a minute. 'Ten miles away,' he said lightly. 'Or a bit more. No problem, we'll be there by nightfall.'

'We should have brought some chairs,' said Rob.

Jay had the look of a man just barely resisting the temptation to roll his eyes. I didn't blame him. Four chairs, large enough to fly in without falling overboard, would not be easily portable. He set off down the hill, moving at a brisk march. 'Better get going,' he called back.

'Wait, I have a better idea.' It was me who spoke, and by way of response I received from all three gentlemen an identical quizzical look. 'I have, um, a small secret,' I ventured.

'*Really.*' Jay's voice dripped sarcasm.

Baron Alban merely raised a brow at me that said: *Is that supposed to be a surprise?*

I did not try to explain, which might have been a mistake, since my next move was to stick my hand down the front of my dress and start rooting about in there.

'Um, Ves...?' said Jay.

'Hang on.' Almost... ah, there they were. I withdrew my hand, bringing forth a set of tiny silver pipes.

Jay's confusion only grew. 'Panpipes?'

'Syrinx pipes,' I corrected. The baron knew what they were, for his grin flashed bright and he chuckled.

I blew a trilling melody upon my beautiful pipes and in response, a breeze swirled through my hair. Not a frantic, grabbing breeze like the Winds of the Ways, but a gentle wind, warm and serene and scented with flowers.

I shoved the pipes away again and faced the horizon. 'Any moment now.'

'Should I ask why you keep charmed syrinx pipes in your undergarments?' Jay said, apparently more

148

intrigued by that question than whatever might come of my music.

'They're safe in there,' I murmured, not paying him much attention.

If he made any response, I missed it, for there in the sky was a pinprick of colour, growing rapidly larger and more distinct. Three others formed around it. They flew fast, feathered pinions spread wide to ride the winds, and soon they were swooping in to land upon the hilltop nearby.

'*Unicorns?*' said Jay, incredulous. 'You just whistled a quartet of winged unicorns out of your bra?'

'Never underestimate the benefits of a good bra,' I told him with dignity. 'As many a lingerie company will tell you.'

Jay, for once, had nothing to say.

15

ALBAN TOOK THE STALLION, of course, it being the only beast large enough to bear the baron's rather bulky frame. Twenty hands high if he was an inch, the stallion rippled with muscle, his hide almost as gleamingly bronze as the baron's hair. They made a handsome pair.

My own unicorn was white, though her coat and horn glinted silvery in the right light. She and I made friends years ago, and we've been on several adventures together. The second time we met I gave her a name: Adeline. 'Addie,' I greeted her warmly, as she nosed and lipped at my cardigan. I gave her a kiss, and a ball of sugar. She dipped a bit to permit me to spring up onto her back; I took hold of the silver rope she wears which more or less keeps me from falling off, and we were ready to go.

Rob, too, was mounted up, sitting competently astride a night-black unicorn I felt a bit envious of. What a majestic creature she was! Her tapering horn was indigo traced with silver, her mane black glittering with stars. I had never seen her before; a new friend of Addie's, obviously.

Jay, though, was in trouble. There was but one unicorn left for him to choose: a little mare of pale golden hide and rippling white tresses. She seemed friendly enough, but somehow they were not getting along. Jay stood several feet away from her, hands on hips, eyeing her with no friendly spirit, and the mare was dancing nervously from hoof to hoof.

'Up, Jay!' I called. 'No time to waste!'

'It may come as a surprise to you to learn that I have never ridden a unicorn.'

'No problem. It's much like riding a horse, only more... airborne.'

'What makes you think I'm capable of riding a horse?'

That *did* surprise me a little. Who didn't know how to ride a horse? But I suppose the arts of chair-riding, and related charmery, are more likely to appear on the university's curriculums these days. Winged horses and unicorns, like so many other magickal beasts, are becoming scarce.

'What do you think, Addie?' I whispered to her, patting her silky neck. 'Do you think you could carry two of us? We're both skinny and on the short side, nothing too burdensome.' That wasn't an altogether fair way of describing Jay when he was almost six feet tall. Compared to the baron, though, he was a lightweight.

My darling Adeline indicated her approval by trotting over to Jay and halting right beside him. She lowered her graceful form to the ground, and waited patiently for him to notice her.

Which he did, though with almost as much delight as he had greeted the rest. 'What's this?'

I patted Addie's back. 'Join me, and the world will be ours.'

Jay raised his brows.

'I'll keep you from falling off,' I translated. 'Not that Addie would ever drop us.'

Jay was not impressed, but he did not argue. Within a few moments Addie had both of us astride her elegant back, Jay sitting behind me as stiff as a board.

'Try to relax,' I told him. 'You only make it harder for yourself otherwise.'

He tried, with some success, but that was before Adeline rose to her feet again and began to walk. Jay clutched me so hard that it hurt, but I let it pass;

he'd had a hard day already, and they don't issue unicorns with seatbelts. No wonder he was uneasy.

'Here we go,' I murmured, as Addie began to trot, then to canter. She launched herself into a tearing gallop, her glittering wings spreading wide and beating with long, powerful strokes. Her hooves left the ground and we were away, spiralling up into the sunlit sky.

Jay wrapped his arms around my waist and buried his face in my shoulder. I suppose he didn't want to see the view, which was a shame, because we flew higher and higher; so high, anybody who saw us from the ground would take us for a distant flock of birds. Old Winchester Hill dwindled to nothing beneath us, lost in the expanse of rolling, vibrant green countryside over which we flew.

'Open your eyes!' I called to Jay. 'You have to see this!'

'Gladly,' said Jay. 'As long as you're okay with my vomiting all over your dress.'

'On second thought, maybe stay as you are.'

'That's what I was thinking.'

I was glad of Jay's warmth as we flew, for however glorious the April sunshine, the winds were cold so far above the ground. The journey was not long, for my unicorns were fast beyond belief; those glorious wings gobbled up the miles, green meadows sailing by below us as we flew. Nonetheless, by the time we spiralled down to the ground I was frozen stiff. I did not so much dismount as fall straight off Addie's back, landing on my feet by happy fortune alone.

Jay walked about, waving feeling back into his arms and shaking himself. I expected him to look nauseated or petrified, but if anything he looked exhilarated.

'Not so bad, eh?' I said, smiling at him. 'Air Unicorn, I mean.'

He grinned at that, taking me by surprise again. 'Eight out of ten, would fly again.'

'Eight?'

'One point deducted for sub-optimal temperatures. One point for the screaming terror.'

'Unfair. There was no screaming.'

'In my head, I was screaming the whole time.'

'I salute your courage,' I told him, matching action to words.

He rolled his eyes and turned away from me, which was rather unfair considering I had been serious. But never mind. I certainly wasn't going to admit that my knees were a bit weak, too; I've flown by unicorn a few times, but the combination of height and speed combined with the lack of safety features always takes a toll.

'This is the right place,' said Alban, striding up with his bronze stallion trailing behind him. 'Near enough.' The wind had done terrible things to *my* hair, I had no doubt, but the baron merely looked handsomely windswept. Some people spend a lot of quality time with a hairdryer trying to achieve that effect, and without much success.

We had come down in a field, just within sight of a pretty village — Alresford, presumably. I was not worried about being spotted; Adeline is used to passing herself off as a swan, or a goose, or some other large bird, under the cursory glance of a non-magickal observer. Nonetheless, I judged it best to dismiss her and her little herd as soon as we were certain of no longer needing them.

'Thank you,' I whispered to Addie, kissing her soft nose, and she whickered at me before trotting off.

The closer we got to Farringale, the more Baron Alban's urgency increased. He led us off towards the old town at a storming pace, and I had little time to admire the neat terraced houses with their bright paintwork, the tiny shops, or the delightful old timber-framed mill with its crown of thatch. Sun dappled the broad streets, the air was fresh and bright, and I wished we had gone there with a picnic or something, ready to enjoy the day. But Alban looked as grim as death, which was helpful in recalling my mind to our real purpose. We passed occasional strollers and shoppers as we tore through Alresford, but the baron attracted no real notice whatsoever; no doubt he was adept at concealing his unusually tall frame, unusual features and distinctive skin colour behind a glamour charm.

We stopped at last not far away from the lovely old mill. A sturdy bridge arched over the clear water of the River Alre, a blocky construct built from stone and brick. Clearly ancient, it must date, I guessed, from somewhere in the medieval period — a rare survival from such far-distant days. The bridge dwarfed the narrow waterway running beneath it; its pointed arch rose high enough for us to walk right underneath. We stopped on a little ledge next to the water, and looked expectantly at Alban.

'Key?' he said, looking at me.

I withdrew my beautiful key from my pocket. To my delight, the sapphire blazed when the light hit it; was it the sun that lit its internal fire, or proximity to the gate it was intended to open?

Baron Alban took two more keys out of his own pockets: one shining gold set with a ruby-red stone, the other glinting bronze and cradling a stone of vivid green, like emerald, or peridot. Both keys radiated coloured light, like mine, and I was moved to gratitude that we were, at least for the moment, alone at the bridge.

I thought Alban would know what to do with the keys, but he did not appear to. He stepped back a few paces and stared at the bridge, brow furrowed, clearly perplexed.

I could see why. There were no signs of anything like a keyhole anywhere upon that aged stonework. Not even one, let alone three. How were we supposed to open the gate?

'May I borrow that?' Alban said to me, indicating my key with a nod of his head.

Reluctantly, I handed it over.

'Thanks.' The baron held all three keys in one of his large hands and stepped into the water, heedless of the damage to his polished boots. He walked all the way under the arch, dipping down as the roof sloped lower. Nothing happened, save that he got rather wet. He turned about and made his way back to us, shaking his head.

'I thought merely holding the keys might be enough, but no.' He went back to searching the stonework for a clue, pacing back and forth impatiently.

'There.' Rob pointed a finger over the baron's head, at the smooth stonework just above the bridge's pointed arch.

I saw nothing. 'What? What are we seeing?'

'Wave those keys around a bit again, Baron,' said Rob.

Alban complied, looking like he felt a bit foolish. But as he stretched up his arm and waved the keys back and forth, a faint, answering glitter of colour rippled over the stones.

'Well spotted,' commented the baron.

He was the only one of the four of us tall enough to do anything about this discovery, of course. This was troll country, all right. Alban laid each key in turn against the stones until something else happened: the gold key flashed red and sank into the stone, fitting into a perfectly-shaped depression we had not been able to see before. There it lay, twinkling jauntily red.

The baron had no trouble fitting the second key alongside it: within moments, the bronze key with its green jewel had taken up a neighbouring spot, and the two shone side-by-side like early Christmas lights.

Only one key, my key, was left, and its home was soon revealed by way of a sheen of blue lighting up the grey stone. But Alban hesitated.

'Are we ready for this?' he asked of us, looking over his shoulder and down at his audience of three.

'Yes,' said Rob. He looked prepared, his posture confident, his manner composed. But so he always did. I have never seen Rob at a loss, or afraid.

'I am,' said Jay, though he looked and sounded less certain than Rob.

'Onward,' I said, and tried to sound staunch and imperturbable. Was I ready? How could you be prepared for something you could not predict?

This was no time for doubts, for the baron nodded his acknowledgement of our enthusiasm and reached up to place the third key.

Rather a lot happened.

First, the light. If the keys had shone brightly before, now they fairly blazed, and a rainbow raced, swift and glittering, over the arch of the bridge.

The bridge shuddered under some force we could neither see nor feel, shedding earth and stone dust into the water. I winced, suddenly anxious, for the bridge was irreplaceable; what if the passage of centuries had weakened it? What if it was no longer capable of bearing the pressure of the Farringale enchantments, and collapsed? Milady would never forgive us. I would never forgive myself.

But it held. The shaking stopped, the rainbow of light faded, and all became still once more.

With one change. A serene white light shone from underneath the bridge, marking the outline of an arched portal. A breeze gusted forth from within, bringing with it the musty scent of lost ages.

The way into Farringale was open.

16

As ONE, THE THREE gentlemen around me tensed, and stared into that pale light with wary intensity.

I didn't. I did not really believe that anything horrible was going to come barrelling out of Farringale the moment the door was opened, nor did it. Nothing happened at all, actually, save that the breeze died down, leaving the air still and fresh once more.

I settled my bag more comfortably across my shoulders, briefly wishing that I had not filled it quite so enthusiastically. 'Onward, then,' I suggested, and went through the gate, water swishing soothingly about my ankles.

The gentlemen let me go first, and alone, which was not very gentlemanly of them at all. But Rob quickly caught up with me, fine fellow that he is, and we advanced together. For a few moments we were walking near-blindly into that cool light and could see nothing that awaited us, which was a *little* alarming, I will admit. But nothing leapt out at us; no unpromising sounds of rapid, unfriendly approach assailed our ears; all we heard was our own footsteps ringing, curiously melodically, upon a hard floor.

The light gradually ebbed. We passed through it, finding beyond an enveloping musty aroma, air thick with dust which caught in my throat; a noticeable drop in temperature, not at all welcome after the warm spring sunshine we had just left; and the silent remains of a dead street.

It was curiously narrow, that road, considering where we were. I had expected more from Farringale than a thin, crooked street lined on either side by high stone walls. Those walls were *golden* somewhere under the caking dust, which was more promising. But still, as entrances went, it did not seem fitting for so legendary a place.

Then we turned a corner, and *there* was the grandeur. The portal we had used was some kind of side entrance, I guessed, for we turned off it onto a wide, sweeping boulevard all paved in golden stone. Ornate lampposts lined the roadsides, each bearing an orb of crackling white light suspended by no obvious means. That those lights still operated appeared at odds with the deathly silence of the city; their eerie, lonely glow illuminated streets abandoned for hundreds of years. Why did they still burn?

Houses of golden stone or white brick were spaced out along the road, set some way back from the street. Each had a wide square of empty space before it, once host to gardens, perhaps, but now as dead and empty as everything else. Pools of still water had collected in some of them and gone green and stagnant; they gave off an unpleasant smell.

Above the hushed remains of lost Farringale rose sky upon sky upon sky. I have never seen sky like that, before or since. It was the deep, rich blue of twilight, though not because evening approached; the sun was high, the city well-lit. Airy palaces of roiling clouds hung heavy above us, as golden as the stone beneath our feet. It was a display of staggering beauty, which ordinarily would have pleased me greatly, but something about that vast sky made me uneasy. I walked a little nearer to Rob.

The boulevard veered gracefully to the left in a smooth curve, and we followed it. Jay and Alban had caught up with us by then, and we walked four abreast, our eyes everywhere. I began to realise something else strange, which did nothing to enhance my comfort: the city was too clean. The passage of more than three hundred years ought to have taken more of a toll, surely; Farringale should have resembled Glenfinnan in its decay, only being more advanced. But the streets were pristine; not even a single leaf presumed to drift over the smooth paving stones. The houses looked aged, but they were whole and sound, not crumbling as I would have expected. I could have moved into one of them and lived happily there, untroubled by leaking roofs or collapsing walls. There was no mess, no disorder. Only the dust, thick and clinging and smelling of dirt and age.

Was somebody keeping the city tidy? But that did not make any sense. We had seen no sign of life whatsoever, and moreover, the city *felt* empty. There was a depth to the silence, a profound hush, that precluded the possibility that Farringale was home to a company of fastidious street-sweepers. Something kept the city preserved — the same enchantments, perhaps, that kept the lights burning in the street lamps.

What any of that had to do with the strange sky was anybody's guess.

'Has it always been like that?' I asked of Alban, gesturing at the sky.

'I've never heard anything of the kind.' He gazed long upon those vast golden clouds, and I saw that his eyes were very wide.

'Interesting.' I was feeling deeply unsettled, this I will admit. But I smothered the feeling and walked on, for I was as intrigued and excited as I was afraid. *Farringale!* My scholar's heart danced with joy at the prospect of so many mysteries, all laid out here for my perusal.

Jay drew nearer to me. 'I have a question,' he said in an undertone.

'Yes.'

I expected a question about Farringale, naturally, or some related topic. Instead he said: 'Where did you get those pipes?'

'That is a secret.'

'Why?'

'Because it pleases me to remain a woman of mystery.'

That won me an unfriendly stare. 'How does that help you?'

'Because I cannot otherwise get you to take me seriously. Something to do with my colourful dress-es and mad hair, wasn't it? How else am I going to hold my own with you?'

'Okay, okay. I'm sorry I suggested anything of the kind. Please tell me about the pipes.'

'Why do you want to know?'

'Are you kidding? You whistled up a quartet of *unicorns.* Of course I want to know.'

Fair point. 'I can't tell you,' I said, and cut off his objections with a wave of my hand. 'I really can't. I am not allowed.'

'According to who?'

'The Powers That Be.'

'Aren't you the rule-breaker extraordinaire?'

'When I have good reason. This isn't one.'

Jay gave a long, sad sigh. 'I have another question.'

'Yes.'

'Why do you keep them in your, uh, undergarments?'

'Imagine you suspect me of harbouring some magickal object of deep and ancient power, and you want to take it from me. Where are you going to look?'

'Bag,' said Jay promptly. 'Pockets, maybe.'

'Bra?'

'Never.'

'Right.'

'Very clever.'

'Thank you. I know that—' I stopped talking, distracted by a flicker of colour glimpsed out of the corner of my eye. I turned to look, but saw nothing that could explain the soft flash of light, the blur of colours I'd thought I had seen. Just the same empty street, and a deserted, white-tiled plaza branching off it. Nothing moved.

'What is it?' asked Jay, who'd stopped a few paces farther up the road.

I shook my head, and caught up with him. 'Nothing.'

We arrived at a wide intersection, and there we stopped, for nobody knew which of the three other streets that opened before us would take us where we needed to go. For that matter, nobody knew what we were aiming for. Our plan had not been a sophisticated one; it consisted of "Find Farringale and search it for clues." So far, so good, but since answers had yet to leap out of the air to oblige us, what did we do next?

I looked long and hard down each street, noting that all three hosted buildings of promising-looking grandeur. 'I wonder if any of those is the library?' I mused aloud.

Alban had a piece of paper in his hand, to which he kept referring after every searching glance at the streets around us. I sidled closer.

It was a map, roughly hand-drawn in biro on basic, white A4 paper. But if I was disposed to dismiss its significance on account of its humble appearance, I was soon moved to reconsider, for Baron Alban's thumb was positioned over the outline of an intersection just like the one we were standing on. One of its four converging streets outlined a smooth curve, from the other end of which branched a tiny side-street. Where this terminated, a blocky doorway was crudely drawn in. All of this looked... decidedly familiar.

'My dear baron,' I said. 'Wherever did you get a map of Farringale?'

The look he shot at me could only be termed shifty. 'The library is here,' he said, and I could *see* him dodging my question but how could I care, when instead of an explanation he offered me a library? He was pointing one elegant finger at a hastily-drawn square on his map, which I was encouraged to note was not far away. Unfortunately, he did not excel at drawing. The library seemed to be positioned about equidistantly between two streets; which one actually hosted the door?

'There are four of us,' I observed. 'Two to take the left fork, two to go straight ahead.'

'Haven't you ever played games?' Jay said. 'Never split the party.'

I looked around at the silent, empty city. 'We don't seem to be in any danger. Where's the harm?'

'Not *yet*,' said Jay. 'But something emptied this place, and if it is the same *something* that destroyed Glenfinnan and is presently decimating Darrowdale, I'd rather take a little care.'

'I have to agree,' murmured Alban.

I looked at Rob. I had invited him to be our Captain of Health and Safety, after all. On this point, his opinion mattered to me the most.

'No need to rush, I think,' he said.

Or in other words, no splitting the party. 'Random pick, then,' I said with a shrug. 'We can double back if we get it wrong.'

We went left. The street narrowed there, and I was intrigued to notice a distinct change in its architectural character. The houses were smaller, and very differently built: most of them were timber-framed, with great, dark beams and white-washed walls. Some few farther along were made from brick, the deep-red, uneven kind: hand-crafted, and crumbling a little with age. They were human-sized and human-built, if I did not miss my guess, and dating from the sixteenth century. I'd seen many such buildings all over Britain.

'They must have had a human population here, once,' I said. 'Look at this house! Tudor, has to be. Handsome, but not too grand: merchants? There was once a lot of trading back-and-forth between the Troll Enclaves and our own towns.'

I don't think my fascination was fully shared by my companions. A medical treatise from the fifteen hundreds might have interested Rob, but a building? He cast it a polite glance, clearly did not see what had got *me* so excited, and found no comment to offer. Alban was focused on his map, and did not even look.

Jay, though... 'It's a shame all of that's gone,' he said, gazing at the merchant's house with an air of faint wistfulness. 'Can you imagine trying to get that kind of free trade and travel going nowadays?'

I could not. Magick used to be commonplace; it was widely used among humankind, and universally accepted even among those with no ability. That is no longer the case. It's dwindling in humans, so much so that it now qualifies as a decided rarity. To those with no magickal talent, it simply does not exist. Our magickal communities have shrunk to mere pockets of activity, carefully hidden from the rest of the world. We survive, and we try to carry as much of that heritage forward as we can. But it isn't easy, and for folk such as the trolls, it's much harder to pass unnoticed.

Rob stopped, so suddenly that I almost collided with him. He stood tense, alert, his head lifted, scanning the sky.

'What is it?' I said.

He made no reply for a while, and finally shook his head. 'Nothing, I think.'

But then I heard it, too: a *swoosh* of air from somewhere overhead, like the slow flapping of vast wings.

'Hear that?' said Rob, in a whisper.

'Yes,' I replied. 'But I see nothing...'

'That cloud,' said Jay. 'It's... is that lightning?'

He was facing the other way, arm lifted to point. I spun around, stared hard at the hazy mass of clouds he indicated. Naught but serenity met my eyes, all golden peacefulness like a lazy summer afternoon...

...and then a ripple of searing golden light, there and gone so quickly I almost doubted the evidence of my eyes.

Wingbeats again, so close I almost felt the brush of feathers against my hair...

Rob backed up. 'We might want to get out of the open air,' he suggested.

'You don't think—' began Jay.

'He's right,' interrupted Alban. He was already making for the nearest building: that same Tudor townhouse I had been admiring only a moment before. He talked on as he walked. 'There's an old myth about Farringale Dell. There was once a mountain somewhere in there, so tall that its peak touched the clouds. And nesting thereupon were the kinds of creatures we do *not* want to tangle with, so, Ves? Jay? This way, and quickly.'

'What kinds of creatures?' said Jay, though he did not argue with the baron: he made for the mansion at a jog.

'Big, winged ones,' muttered Rob, who was retreating backwards, his gaze still locked on the sky.

As was mine, for erupting out of the clouds was a mass of big, winged creatures, all wreathed in crackling golden lightning. *Big* creatures. They were tawny in colour or white, their gigantic wings luxuriously feathered. They had the bodies of lions and long, sinuous tails...

'Griffins,' I breathed, torn between awe and fear. Because if we want to talk about rare magickal beasts, it doesn't get much rarer or more magickal than the griffin. We've thought them extinct for years.

I had time only to register that my frozen-in-wonder awe was sadly misguided, for the nearest of the flock was bearing down upon me with alarming speed, and growing larger by the second... good heavens, *how* big were they?

'*Ves,*' shouted Rob. 'These creatures are *not* friendly!'

He was right, for that marvellous bird's beak opened wide and it shrieked at me, unmistakeably a challenge. An *angry* challenge. Its cloak of lightning crackled and blazed with heat, filling the air with the scent of ozone.

'Shit,' I observed, and threw myself to the ground. Wicked talons missed me by a hair; lightning flashed, searing my eyes, and my dress began to burn.

The griffin banked, turned, shrieked its fury anew. Then, with one powerful beat of its sail-like wings, it renewed its attack.

17

MY EARS RANG WITH the raucous shrieking of the griffin as it descended upon me, all screaming fury and intent to kill. How beautiful it was in that moment, I thought, as I rummaged frantically inside the neck of my dress. What sleek lines, what elegance, what gleaming, velvety hide—

Then Rob was there. Of course he was; that's what I'd brought him for. He was so heroic as to cover my body with his own, making of himself a shield between me and the griffin. How lovely was that? Unfortunately, he also had a knife in each hand. They were the charmed kind: fearsomely sharp, wrought from something silvery and glinting with the light of enchantment. He would throw them and they would not miss. They would bury themselves in the eyeballs of those fierce, glorious, terrifying creatures and the griffins would die and it would be all my fault.

'*No!*' I screamed, and rolled away from Rob. I had what I needed: my pipes. I scrambled to my feet, shoved Rob aside as the first griffin went swooping past, and raised my precious syrinx pipes to my lips.

The melody I played was markedly different from the tune that had summoned Adeline and her unicorn friends. This one began as a sharp, penetrating sequence of notes, a blast of charmed music intended to interrupt our assailant, to halt it in its tracks. It worked. The griffin stopped abruptly and hovered there, only ten feet from me. What a pity that I could not hold it for long! For I wanted to go up close to it, to study it, to admire it. I could sketch it, take back a detailed record of its surprising existence for the Society.

But no charm could hold so powerful a creature for long, even with my pipes to amplify the effect. My melody changed: from my silvery flutes poured a slow, languid stream of notes, a drowsy lullaby, a tune to invoke yearning thoughts of nests and safety and warmth and sleep...

The griffin drifted a while, caught in the grip of a waking dream. Then, slowly, it floated away upon somnolent wings, returning to its nest in those glorious golden clouds. Its brethren followed, and soon the skies were clear of griffins once more.

Rob was not pleased with me.

'What did you mean by stopping me?' he demanded. 'It nearly killed you!'

'I couldn't let you destroy it.'

'It nearly killed *me.*'

'I am most assuredly sorry for that, but it did not kill you.' I went to help him up. He took my hand with poor grace and rose with a groan of effort, or perhaps pain.

'I am getting far too old for this,' he muttered, eyeing me with no friendly feelings whatsoever.

Jay and Alban came cautiously out of the mansion again, searching the sky for griffins. 'Are they gone?' said Jay.

'Yes.'

'Was it the pipes? We heard music.'

'It was.' I stashed them in their usual place, a process from which all three gentlemen politely averted their eyes. 'Shall we move on?'

'I *definitely* need to get me a set of those,' muttered Jay.

Rob was not finished with me. 'Ves,' he said firmly. 'If you bring me along to help keep you from *not dying,* then I need you to let me do my job.'

'I will, I promise, and I really am sorry. But I did not expect griffins. Griffins, Rob! They're supposed to be extinct!'

'And *you were almost dead.*'

175

'Almost! But not! All is well, and nobody had to die. Not me, not you, and not the magickal beasts of legend which we all thought we'd lost centuries ago.'

Rob sighed and said no more, but he trudged on beside me with a weary air that I did not like. He was not as young as he used to be, I supposed, though I had not considered that fact. When I had first joined the Society, Rob had been about the age I was now: somewhere between thirty and thirty-five. He had been all power and energy and a grim kind of competence that seemed immune to fatigue, or pain, or anything we lesser beings suffered from.

But rather more than ten years had passed. Rob looked almost the same as he had on my very first day at Home: tall, muscled, his sleek dark skin unlined, his curling black hair as thick as ever. But for all his ageless looks, he must be nearing fifty. I shouldn't be hurling him around with such abandon. Not anymore.

'I am sorry, Rob,' I said, with more sincerity.

He side-eyed me, still unmoved. But then he sighed, and gave me a rueful smile. 'You're always an experience, Ves,' he said, which did not quite strike me as a vote of confidence. 'Nobody does things the way you do.'

'It's why I am good at my job,' I said hopefully.

176

'True. Nobody else would come out of this adventure with the local population of deadly griffins fully intact.'

I beamed.

'Let's just hope we can come out of it with our local population of Society employees fully intact as well.'

Yes. True. 'And our Troll Court representative,' I added.

'Him, too.'

Alban went back to his map. He walked off with the purposeful air of a man who knows exactly where he is going, calling, 'This way! Quickly.'

We followed, and with all due haste. The griffins might be gone for now, but they could certainly come back. Even I could not have said with any certainty how long my charm would hold.

'Do you suppose those griffins are the reason Farringale was abandoned?' said Jay.

'That would make sense,' Rob replied.

I did not want to agree. If Jay's speculation was correct, what did that do to my theory, and Alban's? There were no griffins at Glenfinnan or Baile Monaidh or South Moors, and Darrowdale was underground. If griffins had driven away the residents of Farringale, then its demise had nothing whatsoever to do with the other Enclaves, and we were wasting our time in coming here at all.

Nonetheless, it was impossible to dismiss the theory. Griffins were known to be touchy, territorial creatures, as we had just seen. If a large colony of them had claimed Farringale Dell as their home, the trolls who lived there might well have concluded that moving on was simpler (and safer) than trying to stand their ground.

Even to the extent of abandoning their Court, though? Would they really? I frowned, unable to make any sense of it. It was all guesswork, whatever we concluded. We needed the library.

'Aha,' said Alban, stopping at that moment before one of the largest buildings we had yet seen. Wrought from snowy stone in great, square blocks, it towered four tall storeys high, and boasted a crowning roof of magnificent proportions. The walls were lit with long, wide windows fitted with tiny diamond-shaped panes of glass. Massive double doors guarded the entrance, set beneath an ornate lintel.

Alban walked up the three wide steps and rapped upon the door.

'I don't think—' I began. I was going to add "that anyone's home", but the doors moved of their own accord and slowly swung open.

Baron Alban gave me a dazzling smile. 'We trolls are known for our hospitality,' he said as he led the way inside. This did not quite fit with my experience of the Enclaves, but I let the comment pass.

Nothing could have exceeded my eagerness to hasten up those steps and into the library. But I was brought up short again by another flicker of colour: something moved in the hallway beyond. Or some*one*.

But when I mounted the steps and stepped through that handsome doorway, I entered a grand white-stone hallway empty of any other living soul save only for Alban. There was nothing there to explain the glimpse of blue I thought I had seen, the flash of gold; just serene white stone and a pair of pale statues.

'Did you see anything odd in here, when you came in?' I asked Alban.

He quirked a quizzical brow at me. 'Like what?'

'I don't know.'

He shrugged, already turning away from me towards one of the great stone arches that led off the hallway. 'Just an empty hall. What else would I expect to see?'

What, indeed? I could not shake the feeling that these glimpses of colour came from no static objects; there was a sense of movement about them, like somebody had just whisked past me. But how could that be? There was no one around but the four of us. That fact was indisputable.

Furthermore, it did not appear that the rest of my companions were suffering from these hallucinations. Neither Jay nor Rob showed any sign of having noticed anything untoward; they were following Alban into the library, leaving me alone in the hall.

Jay, though, noticed my absence and turned back. 'Yes? Everything all right?'

An intriguing oddity it was, and I wanted to pursue it. But where could I begin? I did not know where to look. So I said, 'Yes,' and followed him into the library.

We entered a large chamber with the kind of soaringly high ceiling that can only result in dizziness if you stare at it for too long. Its walls were lined, floor-to-ceiling, with shelf after shelf of books. Books beyond counting, all leather or cloth-bound and looking far too new considering their advanced age. The library had broad, stout, troll-sized ladders via which one could reach those high-up shelves, and a complement of polished wooden research tables, each with its own cushioned chair.

I was in heaven, and clean forgot about the peculiarity of the colours.

All four of us stood just inside the door, staring at that array of ancient knowledge with, I am sure, identical expressions of breathless awe.

'Well,' said Jay at last. 'Next question: how do we find what we need in all of *this*?'

'There are twelve more chambers like this one,' murmured Alban.

'Twelve.'

'Mhm.'

There followed an appalled silence.

'Best get started, then.' That was Rob, of course, unflappable as always.

'*Where?*' spluttered Jay.

'Alban,' said Rob. 'Your map. Is there any indication as to where history books are shelved?'

The baron slowly shook his head. 'I could not find anything so detailed. I hoped that something would guide us, once we got here—'

'Hanging aisle signs, like at the supermarket,' put in Jay, with what I considered to be pardonable sarcasm under the circumstances.

'Something like that,' Alban said, unruffled.

I heard something, then. Not the calm, deep tones of Rob's voice as he made some reply, nor the sound of Jay's boots thudding across the aged wood floor as he wandered off in search of who-knew-what. It was a sound out of keeping with any probable noise the gentlemen might have made: a whisper, a *rustle*, as of stiff silken curtains being drawn back.

Turning away from that glorious array of books, I followed the sound as it came again, and again. Back through the majestic archway and into the hall, across the echoing stone; veering left and through another arch—

I did not make it that far, for someone caught up with me. Someone I could not see, but whose footsteps I clearly heard: the rhythmic *swish, swish* as of silken slippers brushing lightly over those cool stone floors, but how could that be? I was alone in there, or if not precisely alone, none of my colleagues were wearing *silk—*

My thoughts tumbled apart as the world tipped sideways and revolved, dizzily, around me. When it settled and my watering eyes could once again distinguish details beyond an indistinct blur, I found I was... still in that same hall. Despite the sensation of disorienting movement I had experienced, I had not moved at all.

But my surroundings were not unchanged. For one thing, the hall was darker than it had been before, with an odd, flickering quality to the light that soon began to play merry hell with my eyesight. There came odd shifts in the atmosphere with each wavering of the light; shadows leapt across the room, rays of light darted from one archway to another. It was, to say the least, unsettling.

For another thing, I was... no longer alone.

'Art trespassing,' said the author of my woes. 'What will you with Farringale?'

18

THE LADY WAS A troll, no mistaking that. She had features of aristocratic character, finely sculpted like marble, though the fine wrinkles that mapped her face spoke of advanced age. Her hair was all white wisps, a mass of snowy locks artfully curled and beribboned. She wore a gown of crisp blue silk, with lace about the wide-cut neckline and wide, full sleeves. The skirt was very full, and at once I understood the source of those rustling sounds. Not curtains, but a *dress*. She had walked right up to us, and though we had not seen her, we had heard the motion of her skirts.

At least, I had. What did that mean?

I made her a curtsey, for she was evidently a woman of stature — in the sense of rank, at least, if not height, for she was only a little taller than me. 'Madam,' I said, with scrupulous politeness, for her faded blue eyes were fixed upon me with no friendly expression. 'We trespass, I cannot deny, but it is not our intention to disturb your peace. We come upon an urgent errand.'

No response was made me, but nor did the lady interrupt. She waited, impassive, listening.

So I went on.

'Is this...' I began, and paused, blinking away the uncomfortable effects of another flickering surge of shadows and light. 'Am I gone back in time?'

'Nay,' said the lady. ''Tis beyond the power of magick, that.'

'Then what is this? Where have I gone? For I am not where I was *before*, of that I am certain.'

'You have not moved, I vow, save in time.'

'But you said—'

'You are caught between the echoes, and shall here remain until it please me to release you.'

I do not know if I was expected to make any sense out of these impenetrable words, but my comprehension or lack thereof did not seem to trouble my reluctant hostess. For the moment, I abandoned my line of questioning.

'My name is Cordelia Vesper,' I said — judging it best to offer my full name, for to a woman who, I strongly suspected, had survived somehow since the fall of Farringale, the old-fashioned formality of "Cordelia" would sound better than the terse modernity of "Ves". 'I work for the Society for Magickal Heritage. I came here with two colleagues, as well as Baron Alban, a representative of the current Troll Court. May I know whose acquaintance I have had the unexpected pleasure of making?' I ended this speech with a winning smile, the kind that invariably puts people at their ease.

She scrutinised me in silence, not softening towards me one whit. 'You address Baroness Tremayne.'

I curtsied again, a gesture she deigned to acknowledge with a nod of her head. I wondered, briefly, why she had selected me, out of the four of us, for interrogation. Would she not more naturally have chosen Alban? 'We are here to—'

She spoke abruptly, cutting me off. 'Long ages have passed, since last came the footsteps of another in these lost halls. How came you here? What arts carried you past our thrice-locked doors?'

'Keys,' I said promptly, wishing I had been able to retrieve one of them on our way in. Presumably they were still embedded in the side of Alresford Bridge. 'Baron Alban secured two from the Court, I know not by what means. Mine was the third, given into my keeping by...' I hesitated, suddenly much inconvenienced by the House's lack of an obvious title. 'By the House in which my Society is

185

based,' I said, much disliking the awkwardness and imprecision of this designation.

But its effect upon Baroness Tremayne was curiously profound. 'A House?' she repeated, laying just such emphasis upon the word as to suggest that she knew precisely what kind of House I was referring to. 'Say on.'

So I told her about Home, but I had not proceeded much further than to mention its approximate location and date of construction before she stopped me.

'It is well known to me.' She looked at me afresh: less with suspicion, more with respect. 'Your errand? Quickly.'

I did not need to go into great detail about that, either. I had scarcely got into the malaise at South Moors before she began to nod with evident comprehension, her gaze sharpening — and turning alarmed. *She knows,* I thought, with infinite relief. She recognised the problem, knew what it was. She would know how to help.

Baroness Tremayne listened in silent sorrow through my account of deserted Glenfinnan, and the moment I had finished outlining the turmoil at Baile Monaidh and Darrowdale, she came alive — all action and urgency where before she had been all silent stillness. 'Something of a hurry, I find it,' she said, and with a rustle of skirts she turned, and marched away across the hall. I trotted after, followed her into another grand library chamber much like the first, only larger. Jay had already discovered it, I quickly saw, for he was on the other side of the room, intent upon the shelves. He was difficult to see clearly, however, for like the shadows and the light, he flickered strangely in my vision, and moved from place to place in jerky, darting motions most unnatural. He did not appear to see the baroness, or me.

'Your companion?' said Baroness Tremayne.

'Yes.'

The baroness made no move to approach Jay or to talk to him, in spite of her question. She ignored him entirely, and crossed instead to a shelf in a different part of the room. A quick, deft movement; she reached out, selected a single, slim volume, which she put into my hands; then away she went, quick of step and purposeful. 'It would be well to hurry, Cordelia Vesper,' she called over her shoulder to me.

I looked longingly at the book. It was bound in dark leather, quite blank; not a single word was embossed into its aging covers. I hungered to open it then and there, devour its contents immediately, and it cost me every shred of willpower I possessed to tuck it carefully away into my bag, unopened.

Jay had seen something. He was at a far shelf, back turned, reading. Then he was on the other side of the room, near where the baroness had stopped, hand outstretched towards the slim gap in the shelves that had not been there moments before.

Mischief welled up in me, irrepressible, and I succumbed to temptation. As I darted past Jay in the baroness's wake I trailed my fingers over the back of his neck, a feather-light touch which would certainly make him jump.

I did not pause to observe the effects of my misdemeanour, for the baroness was disappearing back into the hall. I hastened to catch up, forgetting Jay in an instant when I realised that her ladyship was walking straight into the far wall.

Not into it — *through* it. This was so powerfully reminiscent of what I myself had recently done at Home, courtesy of House, that I was much struck. Were such arts commonly employed, long ago? I needed no further proof of the deleterious effects of time, the way our magick had faded, dimmed. The baroness was mistress of magicks so long forgotten, most of us did not know they existed.

I followed after, approaching the wall with some trepidation. It had swallowed the baroness without trace, but to me it looked as solid as ever.

So it proved to be, for my face met cold, unyielding stone and there I stayed.

'Baroness?' I called.

Seconds ticked past, and my trepidation grew. Had she simply left, and abandoned me? I no longer felt that she intended to leave me stranded *between the echoes*, as she had earlier threatened to do. But since she had not explained what that meant, perhaps she was doing me the undeserved honour of assuming that I knew; that I could manipulate the echoes as she did, and find my own way out. 'Baroness Tremayne?' I called again.

Her head appeared through the wall, devoid of neck or body; a disconcerting sight. 'Follow, child,' she chided me, and I was too embarrassed by my ignorance to take exception to the term *child.* In her eyes, I probably was, and more or less deservedly.

'I cannot,' I confessed.

Her disembodied head tilted strangely; she was puzzled by me. 'Strange,' she commented. Then her arm appeared, reaching for me. I permitted myself to be grabbed. A swift, sharp *tug,* and the wall melted before me.

I fell through, with a regrettable lack of grace.

On the other side was a spiral staircase winding its way down into some subterranean space. There were no doors or windows set into the walls, just unbroken stone. Baroness Tremayne was already halfway down the stairs.

'Wait,' I gasped, hurrying to catch up. 'Who *are* you? What are these magicks you perform with such ease? They are forgotten now.'

'Not forgotten, while the House remains.'

'But they are not learned, not taught. We know nothing of them, not even at the University.' Her stride was long for her relatively insignificant height, and I had to work to keep up. The air cooled as we descended, the light dimmed; this place was obviously not intended for use by such folk as I. 'I do not know what you mean by the echoes.'

'Spells, rare and strange,' said the baroness, whisking out of sight around a corner; we had reached the bottom of the stairs. 'Dark arts, to the minds of some. They were afeared. No university has ever taught our ways.'

'Our ways?' I repeated. 'Who do you mean by that? How are you here? *Who are you?*'

It did not matter how insistent I was with my questions; they all went equally unanswered. Baroness Tremayne stood motionless at the foot of the stairs, her gaze intent upon something I could not see until I joined her.

Then, all at once, I understood.

We had travelled into the depths of a network of cellars. Low-ceilinged passageways spread before me, intersections branching off into the darkness. The light was so low I could see little but great, craggy blocks of stone stacked into graceless walls, each set with heavy oaken doors held shut with black iron bars. The only light in those cellars was of a faded, sickly character, and its source was no sconce or torch or globe of wisp-light. The light came, somehow, from the floor, and it glimmered and shifted in a way that suggested ceaseless, writhing movement. I did not immediately understand.

I looked closer, stared harder. The floor surged and wriggled in waves of frantic motion, as though it was alive.

Which, effectively, it *was*.

'They are... worms?' I whispered, appalled. 'Maggots?'

Baroness Tremayne shook her head, her gaze never wavering from the mass of pale, writhing creatures that carpeted the floor and the weird light that clung to their tiny, repulsive forms. '*Ortherex*,' she said, and the word struck me as vaguely familiar. I had heard it before, somewhere — or more probably, I had read it. 'Parasites,' the baroness continued. She bent from the waist, a slow, stately movement, and extracted a single worm from the writhing mass. This she held up for my inspection.

I grabbed a glow-sphere from my bag and activated it with a flick of a finger. A clear, bright white light shone forth, a comfortingly *clean* radiance compared to the sickly glow of the ortherex. Thus illuminated, I could clearly see its plump, segmented, legless body, its toothless mouth, its covering of fine hairs. It had no eyes. 'Parasites,' I echoed, intrigued and disgusted. 'They feed off a living host?'

The baroness nodded. 'They prefer my kind, though it is not known why. Inside our soft bodies they lay their eggs. Their young swell and grow, feeding from our heart's energies and the magicks woven into our blood. Such theft will kill us, and swiftly. Then, forth go the ortherex. Their preferred home thereafter is a deep place, dank and dark. Into the rock they go, to drink up such magicks as they find in our Dells and Enclaves, and to find new hosts.'

I felt sick, for by the baroness's words I realised that the carpet of ortherex I could see was but the surface of the problem. *Into the rock?* How far down did that mass of parasites go?

And this was the cellar of the library alone. One building, out of a whole city.

Just how many billions of ortherex were there?

19

To MY RENEWED HORROR, the ortherex on the baroness's palm was by no means content to lie passive. It twitched and writhed, bunching its body into a tight coil, its mouth fixed upon her skin in a manner that to my eyes looked highly unpromising. The baroness winced, and quickly dropped it back into the mass of its brethren.

The thing was gamely trying to *eat* her.

I stared at the baroness, and I dare say my eyes were as wide as saucers. In the midst of my horror, a thought occurred to me. 'How is it that you are still here?' I gestured at the ortherex. 'I mean, it is not merely the passage of time — for you have been here since the fall of Farringale, have you not? Hundreds of years?'

She looked gravely at me, and said only: 'I have.'

'Time aside, then, how have you survived proximity to these horrors? The rest of Farringale fell!'

She turned away from the wriggling parasites and began, slowly, to ascend the stairs. 'Some few of my kind are resistant to the ortherex. Our blood will not nourish them. From us they cannot feed, and so they die.' Her lips quirked in a faint smile. 'Still, they try.'

I thought of the way that tiny mouth had fastened upon the baroness's skin, the way she had hastily thrown it off. Apparently, the ortherex could still hurt, even if they could not kill her. 'How many of you are still here?' I asked her.

'Three, by my life. Once, there were more.'

They were dying out, then, these lingering guardians of Farringale. I pictured her centuries-long vigil, the loneliness of her state here, cut off from the wider world; condemned only to wait, and watch as her few fellows died around her. I shivered.

A theory as to the nature of her longevity was forming in my mind, and I hungered to ask questions of her. But I restrained the impulse. There was not time, now, to pursue that topic. The matter of the ortherex was far more pressing. We reached the top of the stairs, and those enclosed walls now made sense to me. Perhaps there was the outline of a lost door, somewhere inside that walled-off corridor; someone had bricked it up, perhaps in hope of containing the tide of ortherex which had taken possession of the cellars. A doomed effort, and futile.

The baroness took us back through the wall, and paused. How grateful was I, to return to that light, airy hallway after the dank misery of the passage-ways below! I stepped into the patch of sunlight which shone through the main doors, welcoming its soft warmth upon my skin. It was faded and wan in this strange place the baroness had brought me to — *between the echoes* — but comparatively, it was bliss. 'Baroness,' I said. 'Please, tell me you have a way to stop these creatures. Can they be purged? Destroyed? Repelled? Anything.'

A faint smile curved her lips: of satisfaction, per-haps. 'I do,' she said, and my hopes swelled. 'Alas, too late we were for Farringale. But down the long ages we've toiled, and our work is finished. The tome I put into your hands; you have it still?'

Of *course* I did. I took it out to show her, and she nodded approval. 'Therein lies the key. Know that nothing can purge the ortherex once they grow too strong; perhaps Glenfinnan is already lost be-yond recall. But it is not too late for Darrowdale. If you love magick, Cordelia Vesper, then save our Enclaves. I entreat you.'

'I will. *We* will, now that you have given us the means.'

She nodded again, though her attention had wandered from me, her thoughts turned within. 'If but *one* is saved, all is justified,' she mused, and I saw a sadness and a weariness in her that all but broke my heart. 'It will be enough.'

I wanted to ask more of her. Perhaps I could get away with an enquiry after all; just one or two probing questions about these *echoes,* and her surviving colleagues, and the people she referred to when she said *our.* But the light slowly brightened around me until I stood blinking in pure, unimpeded sunshine, and I realised I was alone. The baroness had faded away like smoke.

'Thank you,' I called. Too late, too late, but perhaps she heard me, somewhere within the echoes of lost Farringale.

I stood for a moment, a little dazed by what had just happened, what I had seen. Had I really spent the last half-hour in conversation with a woman whose birth predated mine by centuries? One of a mere few survivors of the disasters that had destroyed Farringale, a mere *three*, who—

And my train of thought ground to a halt.

Only three?

'Baron?' I called, feebly at first. But urgency swelled my lungs, and I bellowed as loudly as I could: '*Baron Alban!*'

It might have been uncouth of me, standing in the hallway of Farringale's library shouting at the top of my lungs. But it was faster than going from room to room searching for him, and that was rather more important than good manners at that moment.

To my relief, he came into the hall at a half-run only a few seconds later. 'Yes? What's the matter?'

I looked long at him, standing there in all his troll-ish glory. I pictured those wriggling creatures fastening their hungry mouths upon his perfect skin, sucking him dry of all the magick he possessed. I pictured them laying their clutches of eggs in his ears, his mouth, his hair; those eggs hatching, growing, killing him from the inside out. I took a deep, steadying breath and said: 'Much as it pains me to abandon this library, it is imperative that we get out of here. Right now.'

Rob and Jay had come running, too; all three of them stared at me. 'You can't be serious,' said Jay at last. 'Not after all the trouble we went to.'

I held up the book. 'We've got what we need. I don't have time to explain, Jay, you are just going to have to trust me. We need to get Alban out of here. Now.'

Rob nodded once. 'Right,' he said, and made for the door. He stood there awhile, carefully checking the horizon, and I knew he was looking for griffins. 'Coast is clear, for now.'

Alban looked strangely at me. I detected a trace of alarm in his eyes, though he kept its effects well under control. 'You'll explain, later,' he said, and it was not a question.

He was as reluctant to flee Farringale as I, but I couldn't help that. He would thank me, once he knew. 'I will,' I promised.

That was enough for Alban, who joined Rob at the door.

Jay, though, whirled about and vanished back into the library.

'Jay!' I called, furious. 'Jay! This is *serious.*'

He reappeared twenty seconds later with an armful of books — books he clutched tightly to his chest, with as much care and desperation as he might cradle his own child. 'I'm here,' he panted. 'Go.'

My heart warmed to him on the spot.

OUR RETREAT FROM FARRINGALE could at best be termed *disorderly.* I did my best to keep the baron away from anything that looked like rock, which inconvenienced us several times, and confused my companions to no end. I had neither time nor attention to spare for explanations.

To their credit and my relief, they followed my lead anyway.

Or Alban's, in the end, for nobody in their right mind would trust *me* to find our way from the library back to the gate. That map of his proved invaluable again. We wound our way back through those beautiful, heartbreakingly empty streets, and this time I barely glanced at the structures we passed, hardly paused to speculate at the contents of those abandoned houses. If Alban got infected it would be *my fault*, and what then? I hoped that the baroness's journal might include a recipe for a cure, but perhaps it would not. She had made no such promise.

For the first time in my life, I felt deeply, personally responsible for someone else's safety, and under circumstances which made it deplorably difficult to be certain they would make it out okay.

I made a mental note not to keep putting myself, or anybody else, in that position.

The griffins, thank goodness, did not bother us on our return trip. We moved too fast, perhaps, or they were still drowsy from the charm I had spun.

I thought I saw unpromising flickers of lightning in those distant clouds as we arrived, breathless, at the gate, but I could not be sure.

We surged through the door en masse, snatched the keys from the worn stonework of the bridge, and watched, panting with exertion and tension, as the door shut behind us. The light of Farringale faded.

Carefully, Baron Alban folded his map and returned it to a pocket in his trousers. It was covered in writing, which it had not been before, and I wondered what the baron had found to make notes about, while I was busy wandering the bowels of the city. He put away the gold and the bronze keys, too, and held out the silver one to me.

I took it.

'I think,' said Baron Alban, 'that it's time for you to explain.'

'*Please*,' said Jay.

So I did.

I TROUBLED MY ADELINE, again, and her trio of friends. They came to us at Alresford, and bore us back to Old Winchester Hill. How comforting it was to feel the warmth of her flanks beneath me, to wind my fingers through her silken mane. It is hard to dwell on darkness, disease and fear when you have a unicorn nearby.

Jay's windstorms swept us off that hilltop and back Home, where we parted ways.

But not without some argument.

'The book, please,' said Alban, and held out his hand to receive it.

'Not yet,' I said, making no move to hand it over.

He stared at me. 'What?'

'I need to give it to Milady. It has to be processed by our library, its contents given over to our technicians. Then it may travel to the Troll Court. Believe me, the Society will fully understand the urgency of the situation. I imagine a copy will be made for our use, after which the book will be sent along to you with all due speed.'

'Nonsense,' he said sternly. 'This is a matter for the Court. We have all the right people to—'

'How many Enclaves are there?' I interrupted.

'I don't know, quite a few—'

'Exactly. Do you want help, or not?'

He stared helplessly at me, and heaved a great, exasperated sigh. 'If that book doesn't find its way to the Court within two days — preferably less — I'll be back.'

His tone fully conveyed what that would mean for me. 'Yessir,' I said.

He smiled at that, albeit crookedly. 'Bid you farewell, then.'

I glanced, briefly, at Jay, whose state was much as I imagined. But Rob was tending to him, so I had a couple of minutes. 'Wait,' I said to Alban.

He paused, one brow raised.

'It is not my place to interfere, but I'm going to anyway.'

That crooked smile flashed again. 'All right, I am duly braced.'

'This problem should have been caught sooner. It's telling that it wasn't. Am I right in thinking that the Court allows full autonomy to each Enclave? That they may live as they choose, according to their own rules and laws?'

'More or less. There are some laws which apply to all our kind, but Their Majesties do take a general policy of non-interference with individual Enclaves.'

'Right. And sometimes Enclaves choose to go Reclusive. They shut their doors, cease to communicate with the Court at all — or anybody else, much — and nothing is heard from them for years.'

'Decades, sometimes. Yes.'

'Yes. So. If someone had made a point of checking up on these people, maybe Glenfinnan wouldn't have been wiped out.'

Alban began to show signs of a great, heavy weariness. His shoulders sagged, and shadows deepened under his eyes. He dragged a hand across his brow. 'Oh, Ves, you are opening a whole can of worms with that one. You have no idea...'

'I don't need to have an idea. I'm just pointing it out. This one's a matter for the Court.'

He nodded and straightened, all business once again. 'I understand.'

With that, he was gone, striding through the door without so much as a farewell. I watched as he turned towards the stairs that would take him out of the cellars at Home, and from thence away. Back to his own world, where I could not follow.

Then I turned back to the others. Rob had Jay on his feet again, though Jay's books had not fared so well. I stooped to pick them all up, stacking them carefully atop one another. They were old and fragile and infinitely precious, and my heart fluttered with excitement. When I took a quick look through the titles, I almost fainted with joy.

'Jay,' I said gravely. 'I love you, just a bit.'

'Help yourself,' he said, with only a faint trace of sarcasm.

'Oh, I *will*. And believe me, Val is going to love you too.'

'Great,' said Jay, and swayed as his knees gave out. 'I could use some love.'

'You and me both. Next stop: Milady. And she is *not* going to be pleased.'

20

LATER, JAY AND I lay slumped in opposing chairs in the first-floor common room. We had adopted identical postures of exhausted inactivity, flopped like a pair of stringless marionettes.

On the table before us stood an emptied chocolate pot.

We had not spoken for a while. Neither of us had the energy, I think, or perhaps our minds were too busy with their own thoughts. It *had* been an unusual week, after all.

But it occurred to me that Jay wore an expression of particular, and deepening, despair, and I felt moved to enquire.

'My first assignment,' he said, as though that explained everything.

When nothing more was forthcoming, I cautiously prompted: 'And?'

'Going to get fired.'

'For what?'

'Disobeying a direct order.'

I scoffed.

'What?' he said. 'You heard Milady.'

'Yep.'

He nodded, confirmed in his woes. 'How long does it usually take them to give notice?'

Like he was expecting the letter of doom any moment now. 'In your case,' I told him, 'I'd say you'll be losing your job in about fifty years. More, if you eat right and exercise regularly.'

He blinked at me. '*You heard Milady.*'

I had indeed. And it was fair to say that Milady was not at her most delighted with us. She had not been outright angry; that was not her way. But there had been a crispness to her tone, a certain air of cool, brisk efficiency not characteristic of her, which was only apparent when she was displeased. Despite his inexperience with Milady, Jay had certainly picked up on that.

On the other hand...

'See that?' I said, pointing to the shining chocolate pot.

Jay's frown deepened. 'The pot? Yes. I see it.'

'Means we've done well.'

'But—' Jay began.

I cut him off. 'No. It *always* means we've done well. If you've underperformed but given it your best shot, you'll probably get tea. Good tea. Or coffee, if that's your preference. If you've really screwed up and it's genuinely your fault, well... I once heard of somebody getting a bowl of stagnant rainwater.'

Jay grimaced. 'Harsh.'

'Not really, he was a prat. But you see my point.'

Slightly, slowly, Jay shook his head.

I tried again.

'We *did* disobey a direct order. And Milady can in no way endorse our actions because she *is* our boss, and no employer alive wants to encourage a regular display of such outright disobedience. But we had due reason, and she knows that now.'

I recalled the high points of the conversation well.

'How did you get the key, Cordelia?' Milady had said (like a displeased parent, she resorted to my true, full name when she was unhappy with me).

'The House gave it to me,' I'd replied.

Prior to that moment, she had been all cool displeasure. That disclosure was the turning point. The chill in her manner did not noticeably dissipate, but I'd been able to recount the outcome of our journey without interruption.

And the chocolate had been waiting for us, upon our descent.

'I suppose,' said Jay dubiously.

'Due reason,' I repeated. 'And the support of the House, which is by no means inconsequential. On top of which, we came back from Farringale alive, without leaving the place a smoking wreck behind us, and with the means secured to help Darrowdale and South Moors and the rest. The chocolate is Milady's way of acknowledging our blinding heroism, without having to go so far as to own herself mistaken, or to congratulate us upon our disobedience.'

Jay began to look more hopeful. He sat up a bit. 'Maybe you're right.'

'I am,' I said serenely. 'You're not getting fired, because by consequence of being my partner in crime, you're the hero of several Troll Enclaves. And who knows! Maybe Farringale can be restored.'

'Maybe.' Jay was dubious, and I didn't blame him. He hadn't seen what I had seen at the lost Troll Court, but my account of it had been graphic enough.

Nonetheless. Milady had given orders that the book, or at least its contents, were to be put into Orlando's hands without a moment's delay — orders which I had been absolutely delighted to perform. Orlando is a genius, there is no other word to describe him. He and his technicians would blend the contents of Baroness Tremayne's book with the very best that the modern world had to offer, and come up with... well, a miracle. Maybe.

Copies of the book were also slated to go out to some of the other teams — Rob's, for one. There *was* a cure in there. It was not described as being fully effective in all cases, and some of the trolls we had seen would undoubtedly be too far gone for help. But some could be saved. South Moors would survive, and there was hope for Darrowdale and Baile Monaidh. While Jay and I lay, inert and weary, in our matching arm-chairs, many of our colleagues were preparing to depart the House for the days, weeks or months necessary to pull the Enclaves back from the brink of destruction. In this, I had no doubt they would be joined by the Troll Court's best — led, in all likelihood, by Baron Alban.

Silence fell again, for a little while. It was broken by Jay, who said, with the randomness of a man emerging from deep reflection: 'I am glad we did it.'

'Me too,' I fervently agreed. 'Not least because of those books! A hero on two counts, Jay! I told you Valerie would adore you.'

She really had. Assuming at first that the theft — er, *retrieval* — of the books had to be my doing, she had showered me with such delicious praise and affection, I had been reluctant to admit that I'd had nothing to do with it, thereby transferring all her heart-warming admiration onto Jay. But it was deserved. 'You are her new favourite person.'

'Next to you, perhaps.'

'You're my new favourite person, too,' I said, letting this pass.

His head tilted, and he regarded me thoughtfully. 'Am I?'

'Assuredly.'

A faint grin followed, tentatively mischievous. 'I thought that was the baron.'

I thought about that. 'He does have excellent hair,' I had to concede.

'He was asking me questions about you. While you were off in the library's cellars.'

'Oh?' I sat up, too, my interest decidedly piqued. 'Like what?'

'Just, general stuff about you. How well I knew you, what kind of a person you are. I got the impression...' He hesitated.

'Go on.'

'I thought he might be angling for information on whether or not you're involved with anyone.'

Aha. 'What did you tell him?'

'Nothing. I have no actual insights on that point myself.'

That went some way towards explaining the text I'd received from Alban an hour or so earlier. Our brief conversation went like this:

Alban: *Will take time to sort out this mess, but how about coffee after?*

Me: *Make it tea?*

Alban: :)

So, I would be seeing the baron again.

Jay waited, leaving space for me to respond, but I chose not to. After a while, he hauled himself out of his chair with a groan, saying, 'I don't care what time it is, I am going to bed.'

'Good plan.'

He paused on his way past, and looked down at me with a slight frown. 'Ves.'

'Yes.'

'Thanks for being a bad influence.'

He sounded sincere, but with the frown? I couldn't tell, so I decided to take it at face value. 'You're more than welcome.'

Jay nodded, apparently satisfied, and dragged himself to the door. 'No doubt you'll get us into plenty more trouble,' he called back. As he vanished into the corridor beyond, I heard him say, distantly: 'Hopefully the heroic kind.'

I could be relied upon to do the former, most certainly. Whether it would also be the latter, who knew?

IT LATER PROVED, HOWEVER, that Jay is more than capable of making trouble all on his own. He doesn't even need my help.

Halfway through the following morning, he and I were called to Milady's tower. House and I had been on the best of terms since I had returned the beautiful silver key, so it was maybe that alone which prompted it to whisk us straight up to the tower, saving us the wearisome climb.

Or perhaps it was urgency. That prospect made my heart beat faster, and I hastened into Milady's tower-top chamber with some speed.

My curtsey was sloppy. 'Milady,' I said.

Jay, right behind me, made his bow with no prompting from me. 'Good morning, Milady.'

'Vesper,' she said. 'Jay. Thank you for coming so quickly.'

'House gave us a lift,' I said.

'Thank you, House.' The air glittered. 'I am sorry to dispatch you again so soon after your last... adventure. I am aware that you must both be tired. But there is a matter of some urgency requiring immediate attention.'

How intriguing. 'We are at your disposal,' I said.

'Always,' said Jay. Was he still worried about getting fired?

Milady actually hesitated. That is never a good sign. 'Jay, you showed enormous presence of mind in thinking to extract books from Farringale, and I applaud you.'

'Thank you,' he said.

'But on that topic...'

My heart sank with a nameless sense of foreboding — and quickened with an equally nameless feeling of excitement. I exchanged a look with Jay, whose face registered much the same feelings as my own.

'Yes?' said Jay.

'There is something of a problem. Please report to Valerie at once.'

'Yes, Milady.' Jay and I turned as one, already hastening away.

But Milady wasn't quite finished with us. 'Ves?'

'Yes ma'am.'

'Please prepare yourself for some instances of... poor language.'

'From *Val?*' I said, incredulous. I have never known Valerie to use even a mild expletive. But supposing she did, why would Milady think it necessary to warn us?

'You will see what I mean when you reach the library. Go quickly, please.'

We went.

'Gudgeon!' roared a voice as we approached the library door. 'Canker-blossom! Dismal, hedge-born, logger-headed puttock! Churlish, thou art, and full beef-witted! A plague upon thee, and thrice over!'

Needless to say, it was not Val.

As Jay and I burst through the door and arrived, breathless and astonished, in the library foyer, the voice -- a full-throated, sonorous male roar -- took up its insults anew. 'Weedy dewberry!' it cried. 'Idle-headed wagtail!'

Val was seated behind her desk, remonstrating wearily with the voice by way of sentences but half-uttered. 'I meant only that--' she began, but was interrupted with a renewed cry of: 'Hedge-born!'

'Now really, that is *too* much!' said Val sharply.

'Too much for *thee*, lily-liver, and no doubt!' retorted the voice.

This exchange continued, but Jay and I were none the wiser for listening to it, for as far as we could see, the library was empty besides ourselves and Val.

'Er, Val?' I said after a while.

She looked at me with an air of long-suffering irritation, her hands folded tightly around a large, leather-bound book. 'Hello, Ves, Jay. Sent by Milady? Lucky you.' Her words were half drowned out by a renewed tirade from the disembodied voice, which she did a creditable job of ignoring.

Jay gave up. 'Valerie,' he said gravely. '*What the hell is this?*'

Valerie rolled her eyes towards the ceiling, and dropped her ancient, fragile, handsome-looking tome onto her desk, where it landed with a great *thump.*

I had never seen Val so careless with any book, let alone one of great age, and could only stare in astonishment.

But the book did not lie meekly where it had been put, as most are wont to do. *This* book leapt smartly off the desk, took up a position some three inches before Val's face, and began to dance up and down in a fine display of high temper. 'Hedge-pig!' it roared. 'I shall have thy *guts* for such goatish treatment!'

'The book,' said Jay faintly. 'The *book* is talking.'

Val merely nodded once.

'That's... different,' said I.

Val sighed, and put her face in her hands. 'Tell me about it.'

Also By

Modern Magick

The Road to Farringale
Toil and Trouble
The Striding Spire
The Fifth Britain
Royalty and Ruin
Music and Misadventure
The Wonders of Vale
The Heart of Hyndorin
Alchemy and Argent
The Magick of Merlin
Dancing and Disaster

House of Werth

Wyrde and Wayward
Wyrde and Wicked
Wyrde and Wild

Made in the USA
Middletown, DE
06 December 2023

44809842R00130